Letters Lived

Radical reflections,
revolutionary paths

Letters Lived

Radical reflections,
revolutionary paths

Edited by
Sheila Sampath

Three O'Clock Press
Toronto

Published in 2013 by Three O'Clock Press Inc.
425 Adelaide St. W. #200 | Toronto ON | M5V3C1
www.threeoclockpress.com

Library and Archives Canada Cataloguing in Publication

Letters lived : radical reflections, revolutionary paths
/ editor, Sheila Sampath.

ISBN 978-1-927513-15-6 (pbk.)

1. Political activists—Biography. 2. Social reformers—
Biography. I. Sampath, Sheila, editor of compilation

HN17.5.L48 2013   303.48'40922   C2013-905580-0

Cover design: Sheila Sampath

Printed and bound in Canada by Marquis

*I would like to express my deepest gratitude to
Coco Guzman, Shea Howell, Juliet Jacques, Selma James,
Elisha Lim, Rozena Maart, Lee Maracle, Leah Lakshmi Piepzna-
Samarasinha, Nina Power, Cristy C. Road, Victoria B. Robinson,
Rae Spoon, Kit Wilson-Yang and Grace Lee Boggs for being the
inspiring people that they are, and for opening themselves up so
honestly and generously to this process.*

*Thank you for sharing your voices, and inspiring me
to continue to find my own.*

Contents

Foreword by Grace Lee Boggs i

Introduction by Sheila Sampath vii

Nina Power 19

Selma James 27

Leah Lakshmi Piepzna-Samarasinha 32

Coco Guzman 42

Cristy C. Road 47

Shea Howell 52

Juliet Jacques 66

Rae Spoon 76

Victoria B. Robinson 85

Kit Wilson-Yang 95

Rozena Maart 104

Elisha Lim 113

Lee Maracle 121

Sheila Sampath 128

Foreword
Grace Lee Boggs

This book is an effort to reach across one of the most destructive divides in our culture: the isolation of one generation from another. It is a reminder of how much we have to learn from lives committed to advancing our humanity. It also captures the voices of women and trans people, who have much to teach us as, at this time on the clock of the world, we struggle to create a new society out of the ashes of the old.

I have been very fortunate. Much of my political life has been shaped in an intergenerational context. In the early 1940s, I first joined the radical movement in New York City and was called a "young pipsqueak" by my lifelong friend and comrade, Freddy (Frances) Paine. Freddy, her husband Lyman and C.L.R. James were my elders. Though they were less than two decades older, they had been very much shaped by the radical movement in the 1920s and 1930s.

Freddy, who had raised herself on the streets of New York, had been a union organizer, factory worker and waitress. She had worked with Margaret Sanger and A.J. Muste. Lyman and C.L.R., who came of age in the 1920s, brought a lifetime of intellectual probing.

As I have written in my autobiography, *Living for Change,* this relationship to elders and an earlier radical movement was both nurturing and challenging. It taught me that the world was rapidly changing and that, while I could learn a lot from my elders, I would also have to find my own way.

In the early 1950s I moved to Detroit and shortly thereafter married James (Jimmy) Boggs, who had grown up in rural Alabama. Jimmy introduced me to the African American community, where I found intergenerational ties to be of critical importance. Jimmy always surrounded himself with older people. After his own mother died, he continued to visit the nearby nursing home, talking with and learning from his elders.

Young people, of course, were a constant part of our life together. As the civil rights and Black Power movements unfolded, activists from around the country and the world would visit us, discussing ideas, strategies and our responsibilities as revolutionists. They included Max Stanford, Aneb Gloria House, Wilfred X (Malcolm's brother), Robert and Mabel Williams, Ossie Davis, Ruby Dee and many others.

To this day I meet individuals, now grey, who remember conversations in our living room or around our kitchen table. Looking back on those days, I think that Jimmy and I—an older and settled married couple—provided a sense of stability and continuity.

During the 1970s and 1980s, as we wrote, spoke and organized the National Organization for An American Revolution, we were very conscious of our responsibility to younger activists who were seeking new ways of thinking about change.

By the 1980s we were actively involved in organizing against youth violence in the city of Detroit. At this time we became acutely aware of how much the generations had become isolated from one another. Older people, especially, had become fearful and disdainful of youth. Jimmy used to say we were more afraid of each other than our ancestors were of wild animals. As we marched against crack houses with We the People Reclaim Our Streets (WEPROS), we would hear elders say, "Why bother? Young people will only tear up what we build."

It was in response to this growing chasm that we decided to organize Detroit Summer. Inspired by what young people had done to forge the civil rights movement in the South, we decided to call upon young Detroiters to be involved in the struggle to rebuild, redefine and respirit our city. Young people, we said, were not the problem. They were the solution to our problems.

From the very beginning, Detroit Summer was intergenerational. We found that young people were hungry for authentic connections with elders. The Gardening Angels, mostly older African American women from the South who viewed vacant lots as opportunities to grow healthy food and become more self-sufficient, inspired and taught gardening to city youngsters who thought all food came from stores.

This summer, we celebrated the twentieth anniversary of Detroit Summer and my ninety-seventh birthday. We also celebrated the publication of my latest book, *The Next American Revolution*. At my birthday party at the Charles Wright Museum of African American History, we showed the film *We Are Not Ghosts,* in which young hip hop artists, former Black Panthers, women peace activists, mothers and children, people of all ages and ethnicities work together in new ways to create a new kind of city that will thrive as a place of local production, learning, art and sustenance. This new, emerging city is restoring the ties between generations, which have been critical to our evolution as human beings.

This book should open up all of our thinking about the importance of these critical connections.

Grace Lee Boggs

Grace Lee Boggs is an activist, writer and speaker whose more than sixty years of political involvement encompass the major U.S. social movements of this century: Labor, Civil rights, Black Power, Asian American, Women's and Environmental Justice. Grace has worked side-by-side with West Indian Marxist historian C.L.R. James and her late husband James Boggs, an African American labour activist, writer and strategist. She is a co-founder of Detroit Summer and currently works with the Detroit City of Hope campaign and the Beloved Com-

munities Initiative and writes for the weekly Michigan Citizen. *She is the author of* Living for Change *and co-author of* Revolution and Evolution in the Twentieth Century *and* The Next American Revolution. *She has been awarded a number of honorary doctorates for her philosophic activism.*

Introduction
Sheila Sampath

"What do you do?"

I get asked this question a lot, and I often change my answer depending on who I'm talking to. Most of the time, I say that I'm a designer. Occasionally, I say I'm an editor, writer or a teacher. Once in a while, if I'm trying to impress someone particularly cool, I'll say (also coolly), "Oh, I play in a band." I almost always add that I'm an activist.

I've started thinking recently about what it means to identify as an activist. It's almost as though *activist* is a certification you get when you've put in *x* hours of anti-oppression trainings or eaten *x* amounts of hummus at community meetings. I'm growing uncomfortable with this way of framing the community-based work that many of us *activists* do.

A lot of these feelings first surfaced when I became witness to a series of *unfortunate questions* (and their counterparts, the *unfortunate answers*). Most of us who do any kind of political work have been on the receiving end of an *unfortunate question* and many of us have asked them, too. I am no exception to this. The *unfortunate question* is generally related to political understanding, usually well-meaning, most often from a place of privilege and always, *always* poorly-timed, poorly-directed, or poorly-worded. It's the white person who asks you how the racism you face daily is different than that time he wasn't allowed to successfully bargain at the Indian bazaar. It's the settler on stolen land who asks, "What's the point in talking about the past?" It's the guy who wonders why we still need feminism when it seems like women can do anything he can. It's...unfortunate.

The *unfortunate answer* is equally hurtful. It's generally coming from a place of anger and a need for self-care, usually mixed in with exasperation and pain and is always, *always* a way of shutting down a conversation. It's, "What's *wrong* with you?" or, "How could you not know that..." Sometimes, it's just silence. It's the end.

I understand where the *unfortunate answer* comes from. I've given it, too. Many of us do political work *all the time.* And it is *exhausting.* And when we're trying to chip away at gender-based violence or the prison industrial complex or collaborating to work towards reproductive justice and body sovereignty, the last thing we want to do is be asked why any of it matters or answer a question that doesn't challenge us or meet us where we're at.

In the process, though, we can forget to meet people where *they're* at. And that *unfortunate question*, as unfortunate as it is, can be the first step in something really wonderful. It could mean a new friendship or alliance, or capacity- and movement-building for our already over-worked communities. It could be the start of an activist trajectory in another person.

That's kind of the thing about activism, it isn't really a *state* or *identity* as much as it is a *trajectory* or *path*. And we all start somewhere and end up somewhere else and move at different paces. And what makes it exciting is that we never know everything; we're always going to ask and be asked some form of *unfortunate question*, and it's from those that we continue to grow and challenge ourselves and the world around us.

And that's where this book came from; from wanting to understand where people I admire and respect came from, how they came to shape the world around them and became the inspiring revolutionaries I know today. I wanted to understand how they frame their activist processes in the context of their own lives, with the intent of adding a layer of honesty and self-reflection to work that demands the same.

I thank them for sharing these stories, and I thank you for reading.

Nina Power

Dear Nina,

First, some bad news: although I am now more than twice your age, you are basically going to be exactly the same person as you are right now. I know you idly hope for something better, for some sort of point at which you could say, "I'm an adult now!" (as if an adult would say that). I can see this from reading back through your diaries from these years (which I kindly kept, although you should know that for about four years in my mid-20s I was very close to burning them). On the plus side, seeing as being 33 is much like being 15, I would say, carry on! You're doing alright! Stop worrying about pointless crap and pay more attention to the things you suspect you might really be interested in (a free hint: philosophy, politics, writing). And don't think that life will always be as boring as you worry it might be, stuck in the countryside with only the sounds of your brother's drums and some cows to keep you entertained. Before we get into detail, though, and at the risk of meddling with the space-time continuum, I would strongly advise you in the future to avoid at least a couple of people who wish you no good. Unfortunately, you won't know who they are until it is too late, and perhaps I shouldn't ruin it for you as presumably *something was learned,* though what that was, I couldn't tell you...

I sense from your diary entries a certain kind of world-weariness, combined with an anxiety about what others think of you: so far, so teenage. But trust me, something strange will happen as you get older: you'll become much less blasé about things, and the more you know, the more optimistic you'll be. If this sounds paradoxical, that's because it is: don't think you know anything at 15, let alone how other people work, or that your rather Fukuyama-ish feeling that history is over is correct. It is true that being a teenager in the United Kingdom—and no doubt elsewhere in Europe—after the fall of the Berlin Wall *did* have something "post-" about it, with the feeling that whatever this faintly democratic but profoundly unequal political system *was,* it would probably last forever. Although you did try to give it some kind of historical depth, that wasn't really why you felt like that: you felt like that because that simply *is* what it is like to be a teenager in a period where the category does not fold into immediately "adult" responsibilities like war, marriage, children, work. But I wonder if you can use that feeling differently—by reading more history for one thing, and not just those god-awful historical fictions you seem to like so much, where Anne Boleyn would get put in a tower and Henry VIII would roam around being perfectly beastly and eating too much meat. It'd be a good idea to start remembering dates and events so you can make better sense of the world later on and not just see the past as some solid lump of meaningless stuff that happened in a time where people were just not aware that things didn't matter that much...yeah, and that everything had already happened already...probably? If I sound like a hectoring teacher, that's probably because you end up becoming one; I hope that's okay! If not, try to develop some actual skills like painting or statistics or something, because otherwise you will just get left with abstractions and the desire to tell people about mid-nineteenth- century political humanism (go Feuerbach!). You could use all that time you spent doing ridiculously large jigsaws to paint, instead, if only so you have something lightly more interesting to show for your time (stop snarling at me! It's only a suggestion!).

As for worrying what people think of you: that's a tricky one. At this point you're pretty uptight but trying to pretend not to be. The whole growing-up-in-the-middle-of-nowhere thing is not helping, I know. (By the way, despite the pressure your former-motor-racing father, car-obsessed brother, driving-instructor uncle and the geographical constraints of the countryside will put on you, *do not* bother learning to drive: you are absolutely terrible at it. It will take five tests before you pass, then within a month of finally "passing," you will crash your father's car into a lamp post, the curb and a pub in quick succession, causing the police to get involved, whereupon you will promptly quit driving for the rest of your life in the name of the greater good. This will, of course, mean that you'll have to live in places that have a moderately functioning transport system. I hope you can forgive me for that.) But people are alright, in general, and you don't need to be so anxious. You could work on some of your more awkward tics, like giggling too much and trying to pick fights with everyone out of some kind of weird, misplaced form of affection, but then you might be too much like a proper person, and I'm not sure I'd like that (and besides, who would that make me now). By the way, playing Dungeons & Dragons is a perfectly valid use of your time, and actually, the whole nerd thing gets really cool later, so you'll just have to wait for history to prove that to you (there's this thing called the Internet that happens just after you'll read this, but I'm not quite sure how to explain it to you exactly).

You blame yourself a lot for things, and feel guilty often; I remember this feeling, some curious combination of chemically-imbalanced existentialism and the post-historical ennui I've already ribbed you about. But you're not such a bad person, and this guilt is pretty unhelpful. Fortunately, I seem to remember you being angry and funny and silly as well, and this is all very good (try not to get so stroppy in PE lessons though, as you get kicked off court a lot for swearing. You could really use the exercise, though—trust me on this one. If I could get *you* to write *me* a letter now, it'd almost definitely start by denouncing the later me for being so horribly unfit. Please, younger me, find a sport you don't find abhorrent! And know now that lager and Mars bars is *not* an adequate diet for the three years you'll spend doing your first degree). Sadly, you'll find your amazing humour will not always be noticed or recognized. Um, but, I still haven't worked out how to fix that, I'm afraid. On the health tip, try to remember very specifically *not* to run down those concrete stairs at the end of the first term of your full-time lecturing job in 2006: you will fall horribly and suffer relentless low-level pain in your back ever afterwards. I'd really appreciate that. Thank you. And I know the insomnia is particularly awful for you right now, and you drag yourself to school with a brain that feels like it's composed entirely of clouds, but it does get better—especially when you get to sleep beside other people, which has worked out pretty well for you in the years that follow, so no worries on that count either. Score!

Curiously enough, you—15-year-old Nina—don't feel particularly bad about sex or your body. I remember you thinking how upsetting it was that some friends of yours were self-harming, starving themselves, feeling generally awful about their physical existence and guilty for wanting to be sexual. Your intuitions about the culture that permits and encourages this in subtle and not-so-subtle ways are correct, by the way, but carry on not feeling bad about physicality. And stop thinking that novels—especially the weird, grim ones you're reading right now and all the horror ones—are any sort of guide to real human interaction, and please stop trying to recreate situations from novels you've read! That's just silly... And you're right to dislike weed so much, but try to drink less booze: you often create a monster in your over-eagerness to get trashed, and the hangovers get worse and worse. Booze doesn't make you smarter or funnier, nor does it reveal the secrets of the universe, as you sometimes think at this point, but it is curiously addictive and really quite dreadful for your health. I'm telling you off again, aren't I, though really I'm telling myself off, and not even the self I was but the self I am now...stop judging me, 15-year-old Nina! Go and rearrange your tape collection for the fifty-ninth time! Bah...[both storm off]...

So what have I told you? Not so very much: read more history, drink less, eat better, do more exercise, carry on, carry on! But, then again, who am I to tell you what to do? Let me think instead about how I can help you unravel some of the contradictions that plague you and me: you worry that the world cannot be changed, that everything is already ruined. The pessimism that plagues you continues for quite some time, in fact, but it won't last. The desire you have to help, to make things better, to change things for good, can only be—and this is what you don't yet know—collectively expressed. It is this, in a way, that you long for above all else, but your suspicion of groups, of belonging, of, well, being any kind of cliché (let's put it in the way you understand it) is getting in the way. It is, of course, tied up with your worry about what others think of you: for some reason you think that being political is un-cool because it seems to you naïve. But if I could tell you anything, I would tell you that it is your blasé, liberal dismissal of taking a position that is naïve! But again, short of properly reading the history books I keep going on about, there's no way you're going to know this until you have real practical experiences of protest, of organising, of anger shared with others. Just because the country-side seems devoid of politics, apart from those mainly of a highly dubious kind, don't think that politics doesn't exist or won't exist elsewhere. You would do well to think of yourself as less atomised and less isolated. You can look forward to a time where you can discuss Marx every day if you want to! I know, you can scarcely believe what I'm telling you, can you...!

You work too hard, strange little Nina, and you're always worrying in your diaries that you haven't done enough homework, you daft thing. Trust me on this, too: you get plenty of time to work too hard later, and actually you get pissed off enough with the idea of work that you write a short book about it. I think you'd like the book, in fact! I wonder if, in a way, I wrote it for you. What are you reading about feminism? Naomi Wolf, Germaine Greer? Patchily, I think, awkwardly, without much of a real sense about where they were coming from politically. Where did these books even come from? Not from Mum, although she was doing her best to be a hard-working, emancipated woman, for sure, and your relationship with her will be much the same as the years go by. *The Beauty Myth* was something Becky lent you, perhaps, and the Greer from an English teacher (one of the best teachers you'll ever have, by the way). More books will follow, anyway, no need to worry about that…and there are amazing libraries in the city…

So, you get to learn how to step outside of yourself, to some degree. The feeling of inner-worldliness goes away as the years go on, and the gap between your solitary reading and your collective existence gets narrower and narrower. To be honest, you're doing alright, and the more I think about it, the less I have to say to you; really, there's no particular advice I can give you that would change how things go afterwards. Perhaps there is a lot more you could have told me, more than half a lifetime later. You are particularly judgemental at this point, not least because you lack the confidence to believe in what it is you actually like (by the way, later on you do actually get paid to be a critic—a book critic, a music critic and various other things besides—so that particular fantasy actually works out. Well done, young Nina). Do not give up on your desire, as some thinker you come across later on will remind you…

Things get a lot more interesting. So don't sweat the small stuff, and spend more time outside. I know you think it's cool to refuse to learn the names of plants that Mum tries to teach you, 'cos you think it's somehow feminist to be anti-nature, but that's just you being silly. Similarly, your attitude towards cooking is self-defeating! Please learn how to cook properly so you don't have to spend almost all your wages later on in restaurants. But your obsessive book thing is great, and the writing thing is what you want to do, and what you *will* do for much of the time. People, on the whole, are good to you; and you, hopefully, are good to them back. I don't miss being you, but you will hopefully quite like being me.

So good luck to you, half-a-lifetime-ago Nina!

———————————————

Nina Power *teaches Philosophy at Roehampton University and Critical Writing in Art & Design at the Royal College of Art. She is the author of* One-Dimensional Woman *and a number of articles on European Philosophy. She is currently working on a book about the collective subject.*

Selma James

Dear Selma,

Here is some advice from this late age to your early one: I urge you to read as widely as possible, see as many films from different countries as possible, listen to every kind of music. Little by little, you will develop your own discriminating taste based on your own experiences.

I urge you to dedicate yourself to learning languages: know English better, learn Spanish and Chinese and Arabic—the three other most spoken languages in the world. I urge you to start as early as possible so that you can get the accents right and to use the most receptive time of the mind to absorb it all.

The point is to prepare yourself to be part of the world while you stock your mind, so that as you move in the world you can begin to make the crucial connections between the different ways we humans express ourselves. My experience is that we are all saying most of the same things most of the time, and we don't know it because we are locked out of the many languages in which we say it. By "languages" here, I mean not only words, but dance and music and literature and culture and the study of words and pictures and the ways we organize ourselves collectively. I am so sorry not to have the fluency we all need in a globalized world.

And to really know about music and painting and in fact anything, practice it. Learn an instrument, paint, organize with others to do something. Once you try your hand at it, even if you do it badly, you will understand the principles and appreciate the work of others. I wish I had done more of that.

Learn how not to be prejudiced by power. It is so hard to support or even quietly respect—let alone show interest in and work to understand—people and areas of human endeavour that are not respected and supported by the powers that be. And yet, my experience is that it's precisely through backing what you believe, whether or not it is popular or approved of or done by the "right" people, that you develop and maintain an independent judgment, the principles by which you want to live and guide your relationships, and how you want to try to spend your time, which happens to be the key component of your life.

Long ago, I spoke about this to someone much older than I was, and he was surprised that as a young person I had had to work out the principles by which I chose to live. He had presumed that we inherited these principles, that they were handed down to us. But the pervasive principle urged on us nowadays is the survival of the socially fittest, especially the richest—that is no principle at all. In fact, it is an invitation to live bypassing principles. But we need principles because we need genuine relationships with others that are true to ourselves. Shakespeare put notable words into the mouth of an absurd man: "This above all: to thine own self be true and it shall follow as the night the day, thou canst not then be false to any man." The sentiment, in fact, is not as absurd as the man saying it. To be true to your principles is to value yourself and to value the life (which is short enough) you have, so that at any moment you are not ashamed of your acts, of your friends, of your thoughts, of your expectations—of where your principles take you and enable you to go.

Prepare yourself for an international and principled life with a well-stocked mind. I advise it strongly. I'm convinced that if you live your principles, you are concerned about the lives of other people and creatures as one continuum with your own life, and thus you must be anti-capitalist and lead a life rejecting capitalism. That is the most fulfilling way to live. It is the basis of personal relations that are true to your feelings, and it is a way of knowing what your feelings are, and enjoying them, despite the crass nonsense and dross, which for most of our waking hours is poured into our ears and eyes by commercial media and also by what passes for education.

I would love to have been told these things when I was very young. But I must say, having committed to the movement for change, little by little I began to find my way to much of it.

So, don't feel defeated by inadequacies in yourself you will become aware of along the way. Do the best you can. Try to distinguish between those who, like you, make mistakes grappling with difficulty, and those whose aim is to exploit for their own personal gain, uncaring of the pain they inflict. Their "mistakes" are policy—not honest mistakes at all. Forgive the former and fight the latter by any means necessary.

Don't ever think you're the only one who knows or understands suffering. Assume others have similar experiences, feelings and understandings; and try to acknowledge these, confirming your own and others' reality, emotional and otherwise, always looking for allies against injustice. There is a lot of happiness and fun in winning, especially with others, against advantage-takers and exploiters. And, after all, we want to pursue happiness for ourselves, for those we love and for everyone, since our own happiness depends on everyone else's happiness.

I didn't know that when I was your age, but I know it now.

Love and power—we all need and strive for both,
Selma

Selma James *is an anti-sexist, anti-racist, anti-capitalist campaigner and author. Selma coined the word "unwaged" to describe most of the caring work women do, and in 1972 she founded the International Wages for Housework Campaign. In 2000 she helped launch the Global Women's Strike, which she continues to coordinate. She was the first spokeswoman of the English Collective of Prostitutes, a founding member of the International Jewish Anti-Zionist Network,* *and has worked alongside C.L.R. James for the movement for Caribbean federation and independence. She is the co-author the women's movement classic* The Power of Women and the Subversion of the Community. *Selma continues to lecture internationally.*

Leah Lakshmi Piepzna-Samarasinha

Dear Leah,

It's been twenty-one years since we were 16. I know it's a fucking cliché, but it really doesn't seem that long ago.

You are about to turn 37 on Saturday. That is the same age as our mom was when she gave birth to us in 1975. You're wondering if you want to have a kid. I think she's waiting for us, we just have to find some Lankan cisguy somewhere without too terrible an alcohol problem (but what the hell, our dad drank, and here we are just fine) who will give up some sperm in a cup for you. Tamil or Sinhalese, Burgher, Malay or Muslim or mixed are all just fine, as you are a little of almost all of it. I'm pretty sure she's going to be female assigned when she comes down from the stars and your ancestors' lineage to you. You are scared, but you are also pretty sure that if you decide to parent your kid, it'll be about as different from the way your mom knew how to parent you as humanly possible. There will be tight skirts, femme flagging nails, the big old house you live in, lots of your lovers and chosen friends and fam to pass her to when you get sleepy, Oakland sunshine, brown skin. We will never be alone in a house with a kid and your trauma and your craziness. You have around two thousand people to call, but you also have the sureness of yourself. You have the examples of all your queer, slutty, brown mom and dad friends, the ones who have shown you that it is possible to make a revolutionary, queer, brown family in all kinds of ways, them with their perfect eyebrows and ass kicking for their kids and honesty. Your friend texted you last week to tell you she had a dream you gave birth in your car—that curvy, gold, old school 1990 Chrysler New Yorker that is like two make-out couches on wheels, with a disabled placard—and there was a beautiful, genderqueer brown person who loved you there to catch the baby.

Sometimes you get terrified—that your kid will grow up Rebecca Walker to our Alice, that despite all the therapy and all the concrete ways you've changed yourself and your ancestral legacy of violence and colonialism and all of everything more than you could even imagine, your kid will end up hating you. But if you weren't healthily scared of giving birth, especially coming from the line of beautiful, amazing, scarred, survivor, abusive, loving women you come from, it'd probably be kind of dumb. Maybe if our mom had been more scared, more able to talk through those possibilities, things would've been different for both of us.

When you were 16, all you wanted was *out*. I can feel it burning in us still. Every day. Every day I close my eyes, remember and give thanks. We are out. Out of the white house with the black shutters and the windows shut and the blinds drawn and the doors locked and the fence tight; out of the pale, ice-blue room; out of not being able to shut your own door; out of the control of the parents who timed how long it took for you to walk to the mailbox a block and a half down Pleasant Street and waited, vibrating with rage, or sobbing, convinced you'd been raped and killed, if you were ten minutes late walking back. You wanted out, and you snuck and dreamed *out* every way you could—through mail-ordering zines and listening to music, getting every scholarship to every young writers' camp you could, checking out the maximum number of library books, sneaking out to punk shows at Worcester Artists Group, sleeping and dreaming as much as you could so you could access another reality, writing letters twice a week to the first girl you fell in love with and carrying hers in your backpack 'til they were worn soft. I still have them, in a dented, silver IKEA box under my bed.

You wanted to be a Writer and an Activist and have a Community and a Chosen Family and Home, and you really had no idea at all beyond your most desperate wishing and yearnings what any of that looked like or how it worked. That's okay—none of us do. You got taught. You got helped. You had femme of colour mentors who put their hands out—even when you were the you you hated the most, the you you thought was the most embarrassingly nerdy, awkward, ugly, unloved, alone. Amber Hollibaugh, queer, Roma, raised poor, high femme writer and organizer, who you have the femme to ask to be an intern for in 1996, will tell you when you run into her at a grant convening in 2011, "I remember you when you were 19—you walked in wearing big boots and a tiny skirt and slammed yourself down on the chair and told me that you were fed up with working with white queers or straight people of colour."

You had slightly older women of colour and broke-ass, survivor white women who gave you your first job that paid in the double digits, gave you bus tickets, approved your first Toronto Arts Council grant, let you guest-edit a magazine.

You had all the women of colour and queer of colour writers you checked out of the library, who seemed like gods and archetypes to you, who were your role models for who you wanted to be. You met some of them. You became one of them. You realized that none of them were goddesses, that the pedestal you put them on (along with so many) made it hard for them and you to fuck and to love and to breathe. You discovered that you just keep doing things, learning, asking for help, helping, you chisel away at it and things will happen. You discovered that we all want people who show us the way, all want people who look like who we want and dream and need to become. But that you don't want a movement that is about idols, about hierarchical leaders. Ella Baker, Black Freedom Struggle organiser, said, "Strong people don't need strong leaders." Being an artist and a performer in some ways is being a charismatic leader—one needs charisma to be on stage shining for those five minutes to an hour of performance. But you believe in facilitative leadership—a model where everyone's gifts get to grow, to shine. You want to be recognized for your work and gifts, not erased, but you don't want anyone to scream, "Oh my god, it's her!" when they see you. You don't want anyone to see you as anything that they can't be. That's not your feminism. Even though capitalism makes it hard for folks to imagine a feminism or a movement that is otherwise.

You also wanted to Heal, and you didn't really know what that meant except that inside you there really is a voice leading you from your gut, the one that tells you to get as many 4s and 5s on your AP exams as possible, to apply to weirdo colleges, to get as far away from your family as possible. When you close your eyes, you see a small apartment, three little rooms riding shotgun, a door that shuts, colours, warmth, friends and sweet alone. You smell the deliriousness of lilacs blooming in a New York spring as you stroll the streets with no curfew, with cutoffs, boots and a hoodie, your young girl-self walking free, trying to find herself inside her body. You followed the path to the stars in your gut. You did things that probably looked insane to anyone who was watching. Leaving the country you grew up in on a Greyhound with two backpacks, falling deliciously in love at 21 with your separated-at-birth mixed brown queer love you want to smash the prison industrial complex with, getting married in Dufferin Grove Park so you can get your landed status. Healing is not a straight shot, a logical five-year plan. Healing is a brown queer girl survivor's Choose Your Own Adventure. Dumpster mangoes in Kensington Market? Make your own queer Diwali with your two best friends in 1997? Pray to your ancestors when you barely know them? Spend days in silence making herbal tinctures, writing poems on a 1987 Mac Classic, growing collards and raspberries in your garden? Yes. All of the above.

When you were 26, a lover who is still a friend told you 26, 26 is when you can no longer be precocious. He meant you can't just coast on being promising, you have to start doing more, and you took him to heart. That was just a decade ago. You have performed on big stages and little ones. You have lead marches and founded Asian Arts Freedom schools. You have published three books. You're a Lambda finalist. You got a text from your friend in Salt Lake City at 7 AM in the Holiday Inn Express Edmonton where you were co-teaching a workshop about how to transform violence without using the police, and you screamed and screamed and called your lover on video Skype from the bathroom floor. You co-founded an arts organisation with one of your best friends—a touring, floating cabaret of queer and trans people of colour performers—and you have toured North America three times and weathered good funding and grant denials, the years of great press and the year both of you were so angry at each other you barely spoke. You are a lead artist for another arts organisation. You teach writing to queer and trans immigrant youth. Your life is rich. Lately, you have realized you need to figure out how to make a life that is not just about the self-employed hustle of a no-trust-fund brown girl with a chronic illness who makes up her entire life through emails and favours and an immense, interdependent care network. But you wouldn't trade it. You have the word "lucky" tattooed on your right wrist. You are. Nothing is promised, but it happens anyway. It happens because you all make it happen. You—singular and plural.

You have so many friends you don't have enough time to hang out with them all. Hardly. But you still have a life where brunches and eating strawberry ice cream on the beach watching the sun go down and climbing into the canyon on Sundays are part of it.

You have been hungry and scared and broke. You have been off the books with no visa, engaged to an abusive, terrible, complicated person you loved a lot who is your ticket to immigration status in Canada. You have lived on a twenty dollar a week budget for food and transit. You have been evicted. You rode a trike through Toronto pre-greenhouse effect winters with no parka. You have always, always taken care of yourself.

You just walked through the backyard of your rambling East Bay house. Your house is fighting an eviction from terrible landlords, but you are calm. You might buy a house because the market crashed and there are all these land trusts, good friends and IndieGoGo campaigns in the world. You aren't alone.

And this is the point. Movement means you are never alone, unless you want to be. The queer and trans, feminist of colour, anti-colonial, disability-loving, broke-ass genius movement you are a part of has saved your life over and over again. If your revolutionary consciousness was born from wanting to escape your parents' locked-down house, your revolutionary world-altering movement and community came from this radically interdependent, imperfect movement community that is rooted in feminism of colour and Indigenous feminism, disabled organising and broke folks being loud around your kitchen table.

You know how you are almost totally alone, the you at 16? How your parents don't really let you leave the house? How your mom has it timed, how long it takes? How she cries and cries and refuses to talk to you when you rebel? You now have a life where you are on a plane, Megabus or Greyhound every month. You travel all over North America, teaching and performing and lecturing. It exhausts you, and nothing makes you as happy as when you come home, collapse in your sweet bed in the small cedar cabin in the wild backyard, curl up with stuffed sharks and books and blankets, text your friends, masturbate, pass the fuck out. But now, you are free. You can go wherever you want. Wherever the world will let you or you will figure out how to slide through. And you can stay home when you want to, too.

You are about to go to a hot springs resort with your lover for your birthday. You are going to soak in hot water; eat tons of free range meat and farmer's market veggies and all of a three-pack of local, fair labour-harvested strawberries (you are a Taurus, you went a little crazy at the farmer's market, you also just ordered enough flourless chocolate cake for twenty-five people on Saturday); hold hands and breathe under some redwoods; cuddle and read stories; and, last but not least, have truly excellent sex that you will feel every bit of, with someone who loves you like crazy. It's not a fairy tale—you just spent most of last March figuring out if you needed to break up, but you changed everything instead. You like this one for a lot of reasons. When you're 16, they're 11, but it means a lot less when they are 32 and you are 37. You were both abused, smart, brilliant survivor kids. You joke now about who would test higher on the SATs, and you can still brag that you had the highest verbal score in Worcester County in 1993. No one knew how fucked up things were in your houses. You both grew up. This white, gender-queer, crazy poet kid who co-founded a national organization, too, and who also wants to spend as much time as possible in their garden and in the trees, breathing.

Sometimes you both stop, hold hands and close your eyes. You breathe in and dream back to the kids you were, that you still are. You both send them images that this is what is waiting for you. Back to the yous that you were. You both made it. Not everybody did. Everything changed. You still have to change everything.

It would've been great if you'd never started smoking those Camels. American Spirits aren't much better. But you quit five years ago for good. And I get why your crazy, socially anxious, terrified self—who wanted the world but who had absolutely no idea how to be in it—needed a social crutch.

Your movement is a promise. The promise you made to yourself that you would survive, and learn how to do more than survive. The promise that you would create a movement that looked like you—and not just like you, but where all the yous that had been othered and left out by social movements would be able to find a home. Your movement is a promise. A promise that those words you didn't really know the meaning of, but knew you wanted— Home and Community and Change and Healing and Art and Fuck Shit Up and Queer Feminism of Colour and Decolonial Healing— are words that turned out to be so much more complicated than you thought. And that broke your heart. But you, and everyone else, learned. You made better words. Broader ones. More precise definitions. Learned defter dance steps to negotiate them. You re-made the world. I promised you we would. And we did. And we still keep doing so. We have that power.

It's like your new favourite Santigold song's opening line: "Don't look ahead, there's stormy weather... But if we go, we go together." Everything is uncertain, except the probability of storms. But we go through them together. We keep going forward past what we know.

The world and your family might've betrayed you. But I promised you different. And it wasn't a straight road and it still isn't, but it is different. For reals.

This movement is a promise, a promise I kept to you.

Love,
Leah Lakshmi

Leah Lakshmi Piepzna-Samarasinha *is an award-winning queer femme mixed Sri Lankan (Burgher/Tamil)-Ukrainian/Irish writer, poet, educator and cultural worker. She is the author of* Love Cake *and* Consensual Genocide *and the co-editor of* The Revolution Starts at Home: Confronting Intimate Violence in Activist Communities. *She a co-founder of Toronto's Asian Arts Freedom School and Mangos With Chili and a lead artist with Sins Invalid. She is currently finishing* Dirty River, *a memoir,* Writing the World, *a radical queer of color writers' manual, and* Homegirl City, *a graphic novel.* brownstargirl.org.

Coco Guzman

Dear E.

For a long time I have refused to think about you.

I put you in the drawer of the bad, secret things: the things I don't want to know and I don't want to share. Many people don't know, but you do, that I have a whole collection of things too uncomfortable to talk about. You have been one of them.

You and I have a very conflicted and dependent relationship. You are the teen I was, and I am the adult you dream of becoming. We are related, but also so far away. Between you and me there is a name change, a gender change, a continent change, a language change...the list goes on for a while.

Other than these, something else has grown between you and me.

Maybe an ocean, maybe a wall, maybe a fog of oblivion and delusion. Or maybe, and this is my idea, a cliff of expectations and a growing shallow appetite.

Where you are hungry for my freedom, I am hungry for your passion.

The passion that hurts you is the passion that makes you brave. It sucks but it's true. Being 15, you have no other option than being brave to survive.

Being brave means reading stories to your sister in her nights full of nightmares. Not counting the minutes, nor the nights, nor the tears, but holding her tight and whispering in her ear, "Now I'll be your home."

This is silent courage. It lives in the nights and is only seen by the stars.

No eyes to see it, no mouth to thank you. This is the courage it takes to be 15.

The cliff starts when you look for the others to see, and you eat off their words.

When they make you believe that you are stupid, that you are childish, that they always know better, that you need them to be.

When you give in to them in your dreams, when you believe their words measure your value, when you doubt yourself instead of questioning yourself and accepting your mistakes as moments of learning. When you think you are good because they say so. When you think you are smart because they say so. Their opinion can change at any moment, will yours?

One day you find yourself alone on the top of a cliff.

When you accept their ideas of success. When you accept their ideas of normality, of popularity, of worth, of love, of good, of bad, of life.

When you believe in yourself as long as you fit in their system. When you impose this system imposed on you over others. When you do not ask questions and accept quick, one-way answers. When you cannot forgive yourself and you cannot forgive others.

When you think you are the one who knows the truth, you are probably alone over the cliff.

I am telling you this before it all happens. For now your passion and your silent courage prevent you from reaching the cliff. Because you know nobody likes you, your heart beats without them telling it to do so. You use your pride as a loving hug to yourself and you spend your evenings drawing on the cold floor of your bedroom.

One day you'll be on the cliff, and you'll put your 15-year-old self in a sealed box under the bed and pretend they did not exist. They are not good enough for the person you will pretend to be—a name change, a gender change, a continent change, a language change apart. You will keep on drawing, but expect to do it well.

Sometimes we think we become better people when we grow up, but this is not the case for everyone. I am sure there are many times when I am no better than you. Sometimes I wish you could come back, if only for a moment, to scold me and take me by the hand to "waste" my time with you in a park.

There, we will talk about the cliffs, the fogs and the important things in life.

You will show me the passion and the silent courage, and I will tell you some of the things that will happen to you when you taste the freedom that adulthood offers.

I will tell you how good and valuable and courageous you are. By yourself under the stare of the stars.

One of the stories I will tell you involves you being on top of a cliff. This is a physical, real, red cliff and you are 18. You are alone and you start climbing it. When you are mid-way your hand loses grip, the rock breaks and you realize there is no way out: either you go up or you go down.

You are at least five metres apart from the safe ground. You decide to go up, in case on the top there is another exit. You throw your backpack, it hits the rock, it rolls down, it hits again and again, and you think, *If I fall, that is going to be me.* Your legs shake, your hands shake, you continue climbing. Metres away from the landing, the rock keeps breaking under your hand. You make it to the top only to discover there is a vulture's nest and no exit.

Nobody knows you are at the top of the cliff. Only a big bird that feeds from death, a silent landscape and the stars coming up.

Because you are the silent, brave one, I take you now by the hand. I'll be your guide and you'll be my guide. Nobody else will look and nobody else matters. Once there was a real red cliff; now there are cliffs and fog and oceans. We have your courage and my freedom and a bag full of stories, mistakes, dreams, lessons, friends, poems and pencils.

With this and our common heart that knows how to beat by itself, there's no point in fearing failure. "Not trying" is starving alone over the top of a cliff, and we are too stubborn and impatient to wait for this to happen.

We walk down together, hand in hand. The trip was worthy, for sure. Now it is time to go home.

Only the stars look, and only the stars know.
Coco

_____

Coco Guzman (aka Coco Riot) *is a visual artist and zine-maker. They are the author of many zines, including* Llueven Queers, *a graphic novel on queer life in Spanish. Their installation, Genderpoo, has been shown and used by activists in South America, Europe, U.S. and Canada, and their most recent piece, Los Fantasmas, reflects on and honours silenced histories in Spain. Coco's drawings have been published in Shameless, Bitch, Pikara, Art Actuel and .dpi, and their murals can be found in museums, community centres, schools, events spaces and living rooms around the world.*

Cristy C. Road

HEY GIRL

I'm wildly impressed and somewhat jealous, I've got to tell you.
I've noticed you have this knack for ignoring the rest of the world
when you need to. I know, I know—some things hurt too much.
Some things stare you in the face when you ask them not to, and
some things seem as if they will never stop. And it's not your teen
years—it's your Moon in Cancer. Would you listen if I told you
that the ability to scoff at any hate, drama, girl-competition, internalized sexism, internalized classism, and all the ups and downs
of your co-conspirators that press on your self-conscious soul
will, eventually, come? It will just take a few years of experiencing
hurt through your microscopic lens (since your *macro*scopic lens
is doing a wildly impressive job of wrapping up all the wars of the
world, questionable beauty standards and homophobic pockets
of Miami in a roll of newspaper and smacking it against the side

of the concrete building called your fanzine). I want you to know, though, that your hurt is valid. And the planet will offer things to you that, in time, will help. I know you would laugh at me and call me a crazy hippie if I told you what lies ahead, so for now, we will have to have trust; I'll trust your anger, and you trust all the creations that grow from your anger. Those creations are important—to people who, for now, may come off as otherwise.

So, can I tell you that I love what you've done with the closet? I love the pillars and the foliage and the floor lighting and the large bean-bag chair that says "homos only" across it in Sharpie. I bet it feels scary when you troll through life denying that there might even be a closet. It seems as if the anecdotes and support systems flourishing from your subcultural belonging will truly hold a place for you and your identity, but I get the fear. I heard about the girl gang—the Cuban girls who hate on freaks, vandalized Monika's car and made you scared to be out and Cuban. Their words are harsh, I agree. But their words are a product of the shitty world we live in. It's the Catholic needle that's piercing our ethnicity. Our beloved ethnicity that we deserve to have. Their words will mean nothing one day, sooner than you think, maybe even as soon as you can get home. Turn on that Pansy Division record and believe in a future full of punk. Punk is not just a prospect, it's the reality you are living. I hope you can realize that sooner than later.

I know, I know. Mama doesn't let you go out that much, and dudes in the punk scene are assholes anyway, so going to shows is always a three-part episode with a cliffhanger. You are a stubborn one, but I admire that in you and I wish I could be more stubborn in some situations these days. I wish I could be more of a rock and less of an airy flake blowing with the winds of change while tolerating bullshit; because I'm aware of the root of its evil, so I look for that root and try to fight that instead.

I know you know Mama loves you, but you have one-and-a-half years left of "Cuban Family Rules," and the love between you will eventually make more sense: when you're 19 and sitting in a Greyhound bus on its way to Philly and nobody knows about it except you and the punk communities that you're so set on exploring.

With that said, I want you to believe that the heaviness of your closet will subside. You *will* feel free. And when you can see the love that's being exchanged between your family, community, identity and self, you will deal with the resulting drama like the biggest adult in the whole family. Or, at least, a very wise one with a turbulent story and a legitimate excuse to have hidden your secrets for so long.

All in all, I think the routes you are taking in order to find yourself are real, whether or not you question their worth every so often. They are worthwhile and beautiful. There's more to be said about your biggest obstacle, though: that degrading wall between your body and your self. Despite your knack of pulling out a self-righteous and angry girl from your soul, I ask that you try to ignore the punk community's attack on sexuality and promiscuity. It is poisonous. It is a straight, white, male-dominated world, and, as radical as punk may be, the word "slut" is still used in a way that is unfair and wrong. It has silenced us for way too long. And, unless we reclaim it, it will continue to deny us our own bodily needs and functions. Some people are made for monogamy, and some are not (unless, for some reason, it makes sense one day). And that is real, and that is okay. I know you are dealing with this in your 16-year-old way, and I'm not going to tell you what to do because I'm not that kind of future. Our insecurities are really powerful things, and acknowledging those insecurities goes far in starting to tackle them. Unlike many 16-year-olds, you are thinking about it: you are internally processing it when everyone else sleeps; you are processing it when you jerk off. *Score.*

Basically: sex is okay, even if you are not in love. And love is possible, even if it takes a long time to make sense of it. And if some douchebag punk guy gives you shit for being hormonally fluid or expressive, remember this: your queer fist will rise up when you least expect it, and it will be glorious. Glorious, I tell you. As long as you keep the Blatz records spinning, and the Green Day one, too. That has been some journey, huh? You and Green Day, and your zine, and your art, and Green Day's newly proposed interest in your art because you wrote a zine all about them. Aren't you stoked? Because I still am.

So, listen to this: when some punk makes fun of your obsession with Green Day, please tell them that human beings flock to music for tender, individual reasons that are unfuckwithable. Tell them that when you're all in your mid-20s, you will look back at those scene politics and laugh. (You will—even when you're 20 and pretending to not love Green Day because your queer, anarchist reality teaches you a thing or two about major labels. *Oops, I have said too much.*)

And please, do me a favour and remember that Green Day's "Disappearing Boy" is an amazing song that entered your life for a reason. Most things in life do, and I like to believe that you already know what those reasons are.

XOXOXO
CR

PS. You will have a cat someday. You will have many cats through many cycles, so please don't fret about the disconnect you have with Chui. Look at it this way: Yaya needed a little Chihuahua companion, and you needed punk rock, and you both found it without even trying.

Cristy C. Road *is a Brooklyn-based Cuban-American illustrator and writer who's been contributing to queer arts, punk, writing and activism since 1996. Road published a zine,* Greenzine, *for ten years, and has released three books:* Indestructible, Distance Makes the Heart Grow Sick *and* Bad Habits. *Her most recent work is a graphic memoir entitled* Spit and Passion. *She's currently developing a tarot deck with author Michelle Tea, and playing with her punk rock band The Homewreckers.*

Shea Howell

━━ ━━ ━━ ━━ ━━ ━━ ━━ ━━ ━━

Dear Sharon,

I'm 66 now. I've lived much longer than you think is likely on your sixteenth birthday. I remember your discussion with Mike: neither of you think you'll make it to 30. We both did, of course. But Mike only barely, killed at 33 after driving his pickup into a bridge. He survived the shooting war in Vietnam, but the invisible scars so many of that generation carry never left him. They finally caught up with him on a cold night after too much to drink.

16 is a pivotal year for you. Of course you had managed to create a lot of trouble before that day. Dropping out of first grade after three days because they wouldn't let you write with your left hand comes to mind. It took a week before anyone realized you had stopped going to class. You preferred the company of what

we called "hobos" down by the railroad tracks and said they at least taught you the useful skill of fishing. Or the time you slipped out the back window and ran away from home because you couldn't wear your jeans and cowboy boots to Cousin Dick's wedding.

Now I understand that you are rebelling against a world of limited possibility. As a girl child in a coal mining town in the hills, the future is always pressing in, expressed in the oft-repeated phrase about every girl's future: "She found a good man. He has a steady job and doesn't beat his wife."

That just doesn't seem like much to look forward to. Especially because you have a sense that there is more to the world than our small mountain valley, thanks to the library, open to you because your mother insisted they let you read anything you wanted. And thanks to Daisy Fisher, the teacher who got you into debate and introduced you to ideas and people who showed you a very different world.

Still, at 16, on that birthday, you know you have something you will only later come to understand as precious. It seems ordinary, to know that you are well loved and supported by your family, that no matter what, there will always be a place for you with people who care deeply about you. You have a sense of home, of a place where you know you belong.

You understand that love can't protect you always from the casual brutality and common cruelties of life. But you have already learned that it could at least heal you and provide a sense of peace.

It is only after you leave the valley that you will learn what a rare gift that is. Love, it turns out, is something far too many of us are denied.

But there is a sense, even there in the mountains, that the world is changing. James Meredith's struggle to enroll at Old Miss will bring the world's attention to racism in the United States. Meanwhile, we all thought that our world was likely to end in an avalanche of Intercontinental Ballistic Missiles with nuclear warheads over the Cuban Missile Crisis. These events, so much a part of your sixteenth year of life, will foreshadow the passions that would drive you and much of your generation over the decade of the 60s.

By the time you are 26, you will know the world can change—radically and rapidly. You will consider yourself a veteran of radical politics, having spent nearly a decade organizing, protesting, picketing, marching, rallying, railing, hiding from police and occupying the mall in the nation's capital. You—and the hundreds of thousands of activists of your generation—helped pass civil rights, brought an end to war, closed universities, derailed presidents, and shattered the closed cultural constraints of race, class and gender that you've inherited.

Yet, somehow, in your twenty-sixth year, all that effort, hope and possibility will end in a landslide victory for Richard Nixon. To this day I wonder how we let that happen. Watergate, his ultimate undoing, was just beginning to unfold. Troops were withdrawn from Vietnam in chaos; civil rights and Black Power were in disarray.

And you will be weary of the violence. The bombing of school buses by segregationists, of the Sixteenth Street Baptist Church in Birmingham, killing four little girls; the assassinations of Medgar Evers, John Kennedy, James Chaney, Andrew Goodman, Michael Schwerner, Viola Liuzzo, Malcolm X, Martin King, Bobby Kennedy, Fred Hampton, Mark Clark; the brave students of Jackson State and Kent State. The violence of the war in Vietnam and the war on our cities touched all of us in that generation. It caused many of us to withdraw, others of us to become even angrier. You will see some of this violence up close. While in Chicago in 1969, you will become part of a group of people organizing tours of the apartment where Fred Hampton and Mark Clark were gunned down. Never again will you be blind to the possibilities of deceit and state-sanctioned death.

But you will be lucky. In the midst of all of this political turmoil, you will get connected to the Girls Vacation Fund. They will help you go to college and graduate school. More importantly, they will introduce you to a community of women, long before feminist consciousness, that will show you women can be creative, courageous and competent in ways you had only dimly understood. For more than a decade, intense political work will be balanced with long summers engaged in camp with young girls from inner-city New York. In many ways, it will be the wisdom of these women that helps you mature and develop an appreciation for your own womanhood. Over the course of that decade, it will be the women of those summers who drive you to create a sensibility not only of women in politics, but of women engaged with preserving and protecting children and the natural world.

So by 26, thinking yourself wise and weary, you will look for some new political direction. You will never forget finding Angela Davis, recently acquitted of murder charges, and her newly forming organization, The National Alliance Against Racism and Political Repression. It is through them that you will come to Detroit.

The NAARPR held a gathering in Detroit. Angela Davis was the keynote speaker. You will walk into the church sanctuary and discover it packed with people. To your astonishment, over half the audience will have grey hair. Only then will you realize how much of your political life had been spent with peers. We were truly a youth movement then, not trusting anyone over 30. Sure, there had always been one or two radical professors or local elders, but never more than a small handful of people over 30, much less over 60. For the first time, you will begin to understand what it meant to be part of a radical tradition in America, that there had always been people struggling for a better country. And, perhaps most importantly, you will see the possibility that you can create a political life.

Angela Davis, nearly 30 herself, had been number one on the FBI's most wanted list. Richard Nixon called her a "dangerous terrorist." Yet she was welcomed into Detroit by Congressmen John Conyers and Charles Diggs. They gave her the keys to the city. We thought, *This is something we want to be a part of.* Any city willing to so boldly take on mainstream America seemed like a good place for us.

But there was also something about the place that was very different from New York or Chicago, cities where we had previously lived. You will remember the first time you saw the sun set in Detroit. We sat down that evening and wrote a letter to a friend in New York saying that it seemed no matter where we went we could still see the sky. There was a feeling of openness here, and a feeling that we had found a place that could become home.

There was also the very real sense that the revolution might be just around the corner. Black Power was on the rise, Coleman Young on his way to being the first African American mayor; a majority Black city council was in the wings, including openly Marxist members.

So we came to Detroit, thinking we would stay at least a little while. But then we ran into Grace and James Boggs. And so your life changed.

The rhetoric of the National Alliance Against Racist and Political Repression had paled quickly. It was, after all, only a recasting of the old Communist Party USA line and spoke little to the concerns around race and gender that are so central to our own being.

Meanwhile, in graduate school, a woman in one of your Ph.D. classes, Pat Coleman, will say the most astonishing things, raising issues from a perspective you will never have heard before. She will talk about the role of Blacks in taking responsibility for the future of our country, about changing ourselves to change our world, about the difference between a rebellion and a revolution, and about the role of revolution in the evolution of humanity. She will invite you to join a study group, reading the newly published *Revolution and Evolution in the 20th Century.* Jimmy Boggs was one of the leaders of the study circle. Later in your life you will write about him, but not often. You will always find it hard to capture the vitality and love he brought to life. Today, nearly a half-century after the publication of his first book, you still find many of his ideas fresh and forward-looking. Grace Lee seemed always to be inviting people in for dinner, discussions and dialogue. She will give you your first martini and your first real discussion of Mao.

So you will begin to work with Jimmy and Grace; you will become a part of each others' lives.

In the mid-1970s we became deeply engaged in creating a national revolutionary political organization that we ultimately called the National Organization for an American Revolution (NOAR). During that time, we were immersed in the efforts to develop NOAR, serving on local and national leadership committees, writing, speaking and organizing.

Those were intense years. For the first time, as a person of European descent (Welsh, our father liked to say), we were in a predominantly African American organization. The tone, culture and ideas were set in an African American context by people whose experiences were very different from our own. Yet with them, and because of their generosity, you will learn things about yourself and your country that few white folks ever confront. It is a great gift and carries with it a tremendous sense of responsibility to help other white folks uproot racism.

These will be joyously hopeful years as we collectively explore ideas and create new political possibilities. Through the work in NOAR, you will meet people who will shape the rest of your life. Now, forty years later, many of these relationships are still central to me. Grace, at 97, remains a vital political force in all our lives. Rick, with whom I've shared more meetings and projects than either of us can count. Joe and Susan, who are by now my family in Detroit. Margo, who recently died after a battle with cancer, wrote articles and pamphlets with me, including some of the first commentaries on race and on eco-feminism. We shared a wonderfully creative bond. I miss her now, knowing she would love the questions we face today.

I also met Nancy and Ann, who introduced me to women's music and culture, a path that ultimately lead me to embracing myself as lesbian. Through these years you will learn that friendships matter. Ideologies change, people do foolish and often hurtful things, but we have an extraordinary capacity to forgive, to love, to reach beyond ourselves. Jimmy Boggs used to say he wanted us "to be better than who we are." And sometimes we manage it.

It is also a time when you will face a new kind of loss. James M., with whom you will be an intensely intimate friend and casual lover beginning in your college days, will be diagnosed with a newly emerging condition. We called it AIDS then. James and I had been among the first interracial debate teams in the country. Together we had invited Dr. King to Marietta, heard the news of his death and organized a memorial march. To honor King's memory, we went to the Poor People's Campaign, becoming disillusioned and dispirited in the muck of that failed effort. Together we had probed questions of race, gender, sexual identity and political ideas. Together we had shared our most private fears and dreams, in the way people do when they are young and willing to tackle any question deeply and personally. James died within a year after his diagnosis, alone in an isolation unit.

It will be the first time you will lose someone who was not family. The first time you will have to really think about what it meant to be gay in America and to think about the implications of the extraordinarily personal impact of the viciousness of right-wing attacks on LGBT people.

James M. had met Grace Boggs briefly when Grace and I went to Washington, D.C., to meet with her friend Ping Ferry. Grace,

Jim Boggs and I stayed with Carole and Ping every summer on our way back to Detroit from Maine. Ping had started something called the Exploratory Project on the Possibility of Peace. Our work with this project pushed us to think more systematically about creating community and the importance of local work. It also provided a way for us to look especially at the work of women in creating a new world.

By then NOAR had imploded over questions of race, gender and gender identity. Now, I like to think we were out of sync with the demands of the moment, trying to make old political forms fit new, complex situations. Still, it was a painful destruction. But by the mid-1980s we had refocused our efforts in the city.

First, we had responded to the growing economic crisis and the massive plant closings in Detroit by starting the Michigan Committee to Organize the Unemployed (MCOU). In spite of our best efforts, this turned out to be a bust. We could never get a committee of people to identify as unemployed, or to seriously challenge automation or capital flight.

Instead, people came to our meetings wanting to talk about the cheese lines. The federal government gave away surplus food to people once a month. Along with staples like flour and peanut butter, there was a block of orangish-yellow cheese, hence the name cheese lines. You will recognize these food bags from childhood, and you always loved both the peanut butter and the cheese.

What people were concerned about was the haphazard distribution system. About sixty thousand people tried to get their cheese bags on one day a month at four distribution centers around the city. People lined up early, pushed elderly folks out of the way, were rowdy and unruly. Those who came to our meetings wanted a more dignified, organized method of distribution. So before long, they abandoned the MCOU title and decided to name themselves Detroiters for Dignity.

Detroiters for Dignity were mostly elderly women who quickly established themselves as a moral voice in the city. With them we began to tackle what was their most pressing concern, violence in the neighborhood. So when we heard that people were organizing to march against crack houses, Jimmy, Grace, Rick and I joined them. Before long we had organized WEPROS, We the People Reclaim our Streets. For the next few years, every Friday night, we marched in the neighborhood, mostly with Dorothy Garner. After a few months, we had reduced crime by eighty percent in Dorothy's neighborhood and developed ties that sustained us through the rest of Jimmy and Dorothy's life.

It was while we were with Detroiters for Dignity and WEPROS that we became a part of SOSAD, Save Our Sons and Daughters, initiated by Clementine Barfield in response to the killing of her son. Clem became a strong force for community peace and conflict resolution among young people.

Throughout the 80s and early 90s, Jimmy, Grace, Rick and I formed a core that met weekly, if not more, sharing a rich political life in the city. Every summer we would go to Maine to stay with their long time comrade, Freddy Paine, on Sutton. There we would talk, scheme, argue, eat and play together. Along the way, I fell in love with Freddy, too. Her spirit was among the most generous I had ever run across. In her youth she had spent time organizing in the coal towns of West Virginia, so we shared the love and respect for that way of life. But on a deeper level, it was Freddy who insisted that we keep our politics not only human, but filled with a sense of joy and beauty.

Somehow, through all this, youth slipped away. I became middle-aged. In 1992, I was 46. It had been one year since Jimmy learned he had cancer. I had lost my father a decade earlier and was only too familiar with what that diagnosis meant. Jimmy died in the spring of 1993.

In spite of his illness, Jimmy, Grace, Rick, Clem, a few other friends from the environmental movement and I decided to launch a new effort we called Detroit Summer. Jimmy had been pressing us to think about what kind of alternative life, economy and culture we needed to create in Detroit. It was clear to us that the industrial age had come to an end. We were also very much involved with thinking about young people. We said that instead of seeing them as the problem, we should be thinking of young people as holding the solutions to the issues we faced. So we sent out a call to young people in the city and around the country to come to Detroit to redefine, rebuild and re-spirit Detroit from the ground up.

That first summer I met a number of young people who reminded me of you at 16. Julia Pointer, Becca Dorn, Tracey Hollins and Anne Rashid were looking for a way to make a difference, not only for themselves but for the people of their city. Now, they too have become older, yet each one has found a way to use their talents and imagination to strengthen our community.

This year, at 66, we celebrated the twentieth anniversary of Detroit Summer. I can no longer claim middle age. Elderhood is here now.

But these last two decades have been among the best. It really does seem that life gets better.

In the early 90s, even in the face of right-wing attacks on gay, lesbian and transgender people, you will be able to find joy and love. Right-wing efforts in Michigan to turn back the small gains made in domestic partnership benefits and civil unions accelerated. You will find yourself co-chairing the Michigan Campaign for Human Dignity, a statewide effort to respond to these attacks.

In the course of this campaign, I met Lee. She came to one of the Campaign meetings in Lansing. I thought it was terrific to find someone politically engaged. Only later did I find out she had only come to meet this person who shared the same name as her dog, Shea (I had reluctantly become Shea in college to minimize the confusion with one of the few Sharons I'd ever met). But after more than a decade of casual, sometimes intense, frequently wonderfully expansive relationships with a number of women, I was ready to consider something more permanent.

To my good fortune, so was Lee. We are now entering our nineteenth year together. In 2005 we went to Vancouver with our friends Joe and Susan and Sally and Dan to officially, legally marry—at least in Canada. I noted then that if you live long enough, even getting married could be a radical act. Lee has tried desperately to bring balance to my life along with love.

Which brings me to why I have not tried to draw overt lessons for you: I know you won't listen. One of your great strengths, and weaknesses, is that you are stubborn and insist on making your own way.

And that is perhaps as it should be. While I have grown old, I have never been far from young people. I know enough to understand they really don't like to be "told." What they do want is someone who listens, someone who shares and someone who loves them as they are, so that when things get tough—as they are bound to—there is a place to go. I have tried to provide that place for the young folks in my life, just as others did for me, as others will do for you.

Today, life is far more complicated and dangerous for you. I wish we elders could make it easier for you, could protect you from so much of the cruelty and injustice that you face. But in the end, we have to trust that you, like us, will do your best to bring life and love to the world. That you will make your own way. The best we have to offer is that we will be there with you for as long as we can.

As my friends in the hip hop world say these days,
Much love and respect,
Shea

Shea Howell *is an activist, organizer, writer and professor of Communication at Oakland University. She is the author of* Reflections of Ourselves *on women, politics and media, and co-author of* The

Subjective Side of Politics *and* Patterns of Power. *She has worked with a number of organizations, including the National Organization for an American Revolution, SOSAD (Save our Sons and Daughters), WEPROS (We the People Reclaim Our Streets) and the Triangle Foundation, and is a co-founder of Detroit Summer and the BCNCL (James and Grace Lee Boggs Center to Nurture Community Leadership). Shea is a contributing writer for* Between the Lines *and continues to work with youth and artists for community-based development.*

Juliet Jacques

Dear Juliet,

I addressed this letter to your "old" name so your parents wouldn't get confused or suspicious. I know what you're thinking: *Who is this, why is s/he so worried about what my parents think and how does s/he know that I'd prefer to be called Juliet when I've never told anyone?*

If I tell you now that I am you, fifteen years into the future, that should answer all three of your questions, at least to a point. This will probably raise further issues, but let's not get bogged down in logistics just yet. The point is, I know who you are: a boy, just turned 16, living in a small town in Surrey, deeply depressed, desperate to leave school; obsessed with football, music and video games; and discovering writers such as Oscar Wilde, Arthur Miller and George Orwell.

Having made the painful realization that you'll never play for Norwich City for all sorts of reasons (but mainly lack of ability), you're starting to think that you'd like to be a writer—if becoming the next Ian Curtis or Richey James doesn't happen. You're already giving yourself a crash course in queer history via Morrissey, Andy Warhol and others. (So *I* think you're a cool kid, even if nobody else does. If it helps, when you're in your late 20s, you'll bump into two old classmates in Brighton who will tell you that when they moved there, they were surprised to find that all the "cool" people liked the music that they mocked you for liking when you were at school. You always knew you were right, of course.)

I also know that you're secretly cross-dressing at home—anxious each time you've done it that you've put everything back in the wardrobe exactly as you found it—and that you've kept the curtains closed so that neither your family nor your classmates (via the girl who lives over the road) will ever find out. You think you're gay, but you're not sure; you struggle to recognize your gender and sexuality for what they are, and even when you do, you don't have the words to describe them. (I think you're using "drag queen"—which you know isn't accurate as, well, you don't do drag—or "cross-dresser," which is technically correct but sells you rather short.)

What happens to me after I leave school?

Well, the good news is that you get a B for GCSE Maths, so you never have to do it again. Even better news is that, despite what your teacher says, things like simultaneous equations, trigonometry and long division are *never* needed in The Real World. (Just as well, right?) Oh yes, and one other thing: you're transsexual.

What?

Don't sound so surprised! I'll try to keep this brief, anyway. You go to sixth form college, leaving your peers behind and making a wonderful group of friends in another town. (You're still friends with many of them in your 30s, charmingly.) You feel comfortable enough to come out, reinventing yourself as an angry young queer who reads lots of books—Camus and Sartre, Marx and Engels, Beckett and Kafka, all the things that an alienated teenager *should* be reading (especially Salinger, you walking cliché!).

You start cross-dressing in public, or with friends at parties, and this lifts so much weight off your shoulders. You go to university in Manchester, escaping small town Surrey (and ultra-conservative south-east England) for a big city with a history of radical politics and counter-culture. You don't find the same group of friends, although you meet a handful of truly wonderful individuals. And the gay scene in Manchester about which you'd heard so much *really* doesn't suit you. So, when you're 21, you move to Brighton to be reunited with your old gang, try another gay (or, as it's starting to be called, LGBT) scene, and really start to develop, creatively and sexually.

By this point, as you are now sending sitcom scripts to the BBC and drafting plays about the First World War, you're certain that you want to be a writer; you write because it matters, because you think it can achieve some social change, because you think that through your work you might be able to leave the world slightly better than how you found it. You spend years struggling financially, trying to close the gap between your revolutionary dreams and what can be achieved, staying as close to the former as you can. Aged 27, the two main strands—your identity and creativity—finally coalesce. Having tried several different ways to manage the impulse to become a woman that you first felt when you were ten, you realize that you need a "sex change." (Ugly phrase, isn't it? Don't worry, it falls out of fashion, but where and when you are, it's the best term you have, so bear with me.)

So you "transition," as it's now known in 2009. It takes three years of navigating the National Health Service pathway before you have surgery in Charing Cross Hospital, when you're 30. By then, you've been documenting your transition for *The Guardian* website for two years, as well as writing lots on literature, film, art, music, politics, soccer and various other things. So your surgery is good news, however daunting it might sound: none of your family or friends disown you, despite what those TV documentaries that you furtively watch in your bedroom might lead you to fear; nobody tries to kill or rape you, despite what those films that you furtively watch might lead you to dread; and you don't become an object of derision or disgust to those around you, as the newspapers that you furtively read might lead you to expect.

In fact, plenty of younger (and some older) people will tell you that your writing has helped *them* come out to loved ones or to better understand themselves, which goes some way towards making those years of sadness and sacrifice worthwhile. It's not a bad way to deal with a teenage existential crisis, is it?

What happens to turn you from a confused, closeted boy in 1998 into the confident, creative woman of 2013? Well, you'll be delighted to hear, it's *theory.* You don't know it yet, though you'll wish you did, but during the 90s—through all that time when you thought there was nobody quite like you, nobody who wanted both to challenge gender conventions and reject all bourgeois norms, nothing beyond the loaded terms "transvestite" and "transsexual"—there were writers in the United States coming up with radical critiques of how "transgender" people lived, how they were treated by the medical establishment and portrayed in the media. They were asking why those who felt themselves beyond male or female were scorned by the political left and right, and looking into exciting, liberating new gender formations. Most importantly, they developed a new language to express themselves, one which helps you to understand and explain yourself to people around you (and, ultimately, your readers).

But those writers are all in universities, and they don't make it into the TV shows or films accessible to you via British television or the newspapers that your parents read (the *Daily Mail* and the *Sunday People*). I wish I'd known to look up Sandy Stone, Kate Bornstein, Riki Ann Wilchins, Leslie Feinberg and all the other wonderful theorists and freed myself from the gender binary. Of all the writers, filmmakers, artists and musicians I've discovered in the last fifteen years, they're the ones who've been the most important. Read them and you could become an activist, joining the Press for Change Organisation as they fight for gender recognition and to secure the right to sex reassignment surgery (nicer wording, yes?) on the National Health Service.

Or you could become a performance artist and appear at the Transfabulous festival, held in London from 2006-2008 to push the limits of gender in creative, colourful, hilarious ways. (You might end up wishing that you didn't waste your time in AS-

Level Performing Arts at college, ending up with a C and learning very little beyond the music of Steve Reich *et al.*) The friends you make at Transfabulous, in any case, will become inspirations and mentors to you—it's one thing to read about gender transgressions through people like Judith Butler or Julia Serano, another to see those ideas manifested in vivacious personalities with the biggest hearts; people who recognize something in you, who love you and want to help you realize yourself as they did.

All this probably sounds very distant, but you're lucky to grow up with an incredibly important tool that will set you on your way: the Internet. (You probably won't be shocked to hear that nobody calls it the "information superhighway" after 1997.) You'll start—in fact, I think you *have* started—by looking up "transvestite" and "transsexual" and finding people who *feel* like you, even one or two living nearby. This helps you humanize them and realize that they're not all like the ones in the *Daily Mail* or on ITV—conservative men masturbating in their wives' raciest lingerie; or tragic, burly people in floral dresses with stubbly legs demanding that their families and the state bend to their every whim. Later, the Internet will help you realize that this is how certain "radical" feminists characterise transgender people as well, and it will help you to find people arguing against both these "radfems" and the conservative "transphobes" (don't worry, their positions are virtually indistinguishable, so you should only need one argument to deal with both groups).

The Internet will also help you to put together a cultural history, starting with Boulton & Park, the cross-dressers of Victorian London who so inspired Oscar Wilde (via Magnus Hirschfeld and the Institute for Sexual Science), pioneers like Michael Dillon and

Roberta Cowell, punk rock star Jayne County and filmmakers like Pedro Almodóvar or Rosa von Praunheim. Above all, the Internet is where you'll find the political queer and trans subcultures that, both theoretically and socially, first save and then reinvigorate your life.

The Internet is just the start: your friends and lovers will point you further towards self-definition and acceptance. Gradually, you'll see the difference between gender identity and sexuality, understanding them as related but separate concepts. You'll realize that all sorts of transgender behaviour—from cross-dressing to surgery—can be radical acts, used by writers, artists, musicians and comedians. You're already seeing this, actually, as Eddie Izzard makes you and your friends laugh with his brilliant reframing of the word "transvestite," busting the stereotypes. This helps you come out to people by setting more positive terms for you, and it's a tactic that will become hugely important for you.

You'll realize, as much through sex as anything else, that you're not a gay man and that you have to take risks in order to survive—as a transsexual woman. There's some bad news here: the depression and anxiety that you feel as a 16-year-old never really goes away. You will have two crucial realizations about this (for which you should thank Rachel Kaye). First is that during your teens, there's at least a little glamour around feeling so alienated and isolated, which is reflected in your musical tastes. (When you're at sixth form, you buy a Joy Division box set and play it so often that you wreck all four CDs and the casing.) Second is that your hope—that it might, well, *go away* as your adult life sorts itself out—evaporates, so you'll just have to manage it. You do this, eventually, through extensive psychotherapy and the support of like-minded friends, as well as discussing it in your writing. (By the way, one day you'll interview your favourite Norwich player, Darren Eadie, about his experiences of depression in football. Amazing, eh?)

Most important, though, is you will gain the understanding that you live in a transphobic society. You've not heard the word "transphobic" because it doesn't exist in 1998, but it's obvious what it means, right? (Prejudice against gender-variant people, basically.) This changes *everything*: you see that it's not *you* at fault for feeling so detached from everything but your world for excluding you in all sorts of subtle and not-so-subtle ways. It is this that motivates you to find pockets of resistance and to create your own, giving a power to your friendships that would never have existed if you did not feel so oppressed. (It's important to remember, though, that despite your gender issues, you otherwise have all sorts of privileges. Use them responsibly!) You turn your self-loathing outward, identifying targets and developing tactics, dedicating yourself to the fight against conservatism wherever you see it.

This brings me to another disappointment (sorry). The people and places that you expect to be radical will often prove to be anything but. This is true for those you find at university, but particularly for the LGBT activism that exists when you're an adult. Right now, you're consoling yourself with your latent queerness by saying to yourself: "At least I don't have to get married and I can't join the army." Well, guess where the people with whom you identify spend much of their campaigning energy?

This makes sense to you—it's an obvious injustice that people are excluded from these things on the grounds of their gender or sexuality, and activists choose them as they are achievable targets with a tangible result—but you still can't get behind any politics that prizes itself on access to society's most conservative institutions. This is where the concept of "queer" really helps you, uniting gender-variant and sexually diverse people under a revolutionary banner, culturally and politically. (Also, queer people run discos where they play Soft Cell and Stereolab rather than the Scissor Sisters and the Spice Girls. You'll need those, too.) But still, prepare yourself for the letdown of feeling distanced from people whose conception of LGBT equality simply means equality under neoliberal capitalism. By 2010, I hate to tell you, there are thirteen openly gay Conservative MPs and floats at Brighton Pride which smugly proclaim: "I've come out—I'm a Tory!" *(Go back in!)*

So your 20s are tough—you don't have money, you don't have holidays, you don't have serious relationships—but you do have friends, ideas and commitment; and as Quentin Crisp was so fond of saying: "Time is kind to the non-conformist." (The Warhol Factory member and performance artist Penny Arcade will tell you this herself.) In your early 30s you've used writing to achieve some of your teenage aims, met plenty of your heroes and completed a tougher path to self-realization than you ever could have imagined while keeping all of the people you already love close to you and finding plenty of new ones. (Oh, and you've kept one other promise to yourself: you're going to watch Norwich City all the time. You'll particularly enjoy a trip to Portsmouth, but I won't spoil the surprise.)

Anyway, I'll sign off now—I have books and articles to write, and you probably have a band practice to go to, or something. Keep reading, keep writing, keep finding interesting people wherever you can and, above all, keep your resolve—you're going to need plenty of it. I know you will. Good luck, and all my love!

Yours,
Juliet Jacques

Juliet Jacques *is a freelance writer who covers gender, sexuality, literature, film, art and sport. Her journalism and short fiction has appeared in* The Guardian, The New Statesman, TimeOut *and* The London Magazine, *among others, and her Transgender Journey column for* The Guardian, *documenting her gender reassignment process, was longlisted for the Orwell Prize in 2011. She is currently working on a memoir and a volume of transgender history.*

Rae Spoon

Dear Rae,

I want you to know that I don't feel like I can approach writing to you with any sort of authority just because I am sixteen years older than you. I don't believe that people of any particular age know more than those of another one. I can't remember some things you know, and there are things that I know that wouldn't apply to where you're at right now. I do have a few things to say to you, though. You can take what you want from it if any of it feels right. Maybe if you have anything to say to me you can stir my memories towards it.

First, some fun stuff: you will always like Hole and Nirvana, so keep on rocking. Someday you will rock out on a starburst Strato-caster in a purple flannel shirt in Seattle, and a few years later you will briefly meet Kurt Cobain's best friend after his band practices in your friend's basement. These bands started out as community garage rock bands, and encountering things associated with them is not as far reaching as it feels in your parents' basement in Calgary. Keep playing guitar. Meet a lot of people. Travel.

Being a nerd is something that will pay off for you in the end. Not being invited to high school parties until your late teens and not being included in the popular crowd will offer you a reprieve from the inevitable amount of further trauma that you might have incurred. Be proud of who you are. Eventually, the glasses and clothes you are wearing may come into style. If you learn to like yourself, other people will follow suit. Confidence is more important than normality.

This is the last year you will have to live with your father. You are still striking out at a man who every day has tried to destroy every part of you. He sleeps in the same house and he runs your life. Even though it's the hardest thing to do, you need to wait this out. In December 1996 you will move to your grandma's house and make the turning point from accumulating abuse to learning how to survive in its wake. When he's gone you will continue to fight him, only he will be in your dreams and fears far more often than he turns up at your shows. You can use your anger to survive until you find other ways to deal with it. All I can say about this is that you are bigger than him. You will outlive the abuse. You will adapt to use the hard things as your strengths. I wish I could show up and take you away from there, but you sister needs you and so do your brothers. The things you are going through now will shape the rest of your life, but after many years of struggling you do eventually learn how to trust people and have a home.

The first time you drink, everything will go quiet in your head. You will use drinking as an escape for the next six years. You find your way into and out of addiction young. I am not saying any of this to shame you or scare you. You are drinking to survive and who knows if you would have without it. I guess I'm not saying you should stop, because going through a bought of alcoholism will make you develop a later sensitivity for the methods people use to deal with childhood abuse. Maybe the only thing I want to say about it is to pay attention to what happens right before you feel the need to get loaded. What are the things you can't handle and how can you find new ways to face them?

Your sister seemed very different from you earlier in your childhood. Now she seems much better at being assigned female, at least from your perspective. This does not make her weaker or less able than you. The same is true for all more feminine people. Her inability to climb trees and unwillingness to play road hockey is no indication of her capabilities. She will grow up to be one of the strongest people that you know, and the thing that you are the most scared of telling her now will become an alliance when she comes out to you as queer in less than two years. The gap between you is a lot smaller than it appears, so maybe you could try harder now to bridge it.

Sexism is something that will affect you at an early age but that you won't completely verbalize until your mid-20s. You will feel pressures, both subtle and obvious, at every point in your childhood to act more "like a girl." You find this pressure stupid a lot of the time, but you recoil from the word feminism as you are taught to. You don't have to wear it on a t-shirt quite yet, but know it is the name for the thing that pushes you to question why you are not supposed to play hockey or solo on the guitar. It pushes you to do a lot of things and eventually makes you do things you might not otherwise have done.

On the subject of being very boyish: you are starting to buy your first pairs of men's underwear and you will soon give up on hiding them from your mother. She will pull them out of the washing machine, give you a prolonged, confused look and then never mention them again. Your hair is shoulder-length but will soon be shaved to the scalp. After you tell her it cools you down in the summer, your mother will line you up with your brothers in the back yard of the duplex and shave all of your heads at the same time. You should feel proud of your ability to move outside of the gender role you were assigned. It doesn't feel like a choice. You never were very good at being feminine, and this discomfort will make a lot more sense later on.

When you're 19 you will meet the first person who you know to be transgender and who identifies as male. The option of being a boy suddenly seems to be the obvious one, now that there is a choice to be made. Try not to run so far to that side before really thinking about it. Sexism will also affect you there, when you turn out to be a very small, not so "manly," male-identified person. Eventually you will regard gender as a huge social joke and wholeheartedly retire from bothering with it. I don't want to make you feel like you need to speed towards this. The process and the years involved are integral to the changes that will happen, and there is no way around it. You are just going to have to live through it.

You are still a Christian. I know you recently took your bible to school, not only to keep in your locker, but also to read as your book for free-reading time in English. You just finished taking a Mandarin course because you think you might like to be a missionary in China. There are many reasons why this is extremely misguided and is not going to happen. This will later on be a large source of embarrassment for you and a good example of the colonial racism that pervaded your upbringing. It's funny how you think you can save people when you're the one who needs saving. One last bout of religious fervor is your final attempt at externalizing your problems using Jesus. I would encourage you to look closer at the ideas that the church has planted in you, because they are the real problems you will have deal with. By this point you know that you like girls and you've noticed that you are not attracted to boys in the same way. The shame you feel is what you really need to worry about.

Part of being white in Calgary is the fact that you never have to fully realize your privilege. You don't have to think about your whiteness, whilst the people of colour around you are made to think about their race constantly. Racism is a word you know but haven't really thought enough about to find the ways you enact it.

Your childhood was full of racial slurs and confusing messages, like when your grandmother tells you that she doesn't believe that people of different races should marry because it "confuses their children." At the same time, her favourite brother-in-law is Asian, and she is very close with that sister and her arguably far more functional family. Your uncles always go out of their way to make racist jokes at family holidays whether or not people of colour are present in the room. You know better than to do this by the time you are a teenager but will still tell Catholic and Sikh peers alike that they are going to hell for not being "born again" or for believing in more than one god. Don't forget these moments. Face the racist things you have said. You were oppressed on some levels, but on others you were and are an oppressor. Most of all, dealing with your own racism is not about your own guilt or taking up more space; it's about engaging with how oppression works.

Your first relationship will begin six months from now. You will meet a beautiful South Asian girl in Career and Life Management class and will try not to fall in love with her like you almost did with your last "best friend." Eventually dating, you are both aware of racial differences, but you will make many mistakes. The overarching external homophobia you face will get the most attention. The relationship is a great success in pushing you both forward to deal with homophobia and sexuality. However, trying to strike out at one type of oppression doesn't negate the presence of another. Some of your most painful and deepest regrets will be your ignorance of racism and how it affects the person who is your first true love in life. You not only struggle at being an ally when your family says unforgivably racist things, but you say racist things to her yourself. Please don't gloss over these moments in your memory or avoid them for the sake of comfort. See racism within yourself, listen when you are told you are oppressing people and try to change it. You will never stop being the oppressor in this context, but this is the path towards being an ally and trying to make more space for people of colour.

Your whole family has always voted for the Conservative Party. You will end up *feeling* rather than *thinking* your way out of this learned loyalty, the first moment of this process being when your future girlfriend has to explain to you why it would be problematic for you to be queer and continue supporting it. Listen to her! She's had experiences you have never had.

Anyway, make sure you vote in every possible election. You will falter at the beginning of being eligible and then face absurd choices like voting left in Alberta (arguably an existential exercise) and later on voting for the less xenophobic sovereigntist party in Québec provincial elections when you don't speak more than ten words of French. Regardless, the Conservatives and all of their children are voting. So, you must try to match them and encourage other people to vote as well. Democracy is still about choosing a group of elites to rule the country, but you can at least try to have a say in which group of elites it's going to be. Ongoing colonialism is still the driving force behind Canadian politics, but there's a huge difference in how political parties attend to anti-oppression issues. No party is perfect, but allowing the Conservatives to be elected by not voting means that Canada moves towards the atmosphere in Alberta that you want to run from right now.

About your music: you are right to spend all of your time on it. Despite what adults tell you, skipping class to practice guitar is actually a really good life plan. By forgoing university you will manage to launch a slow-burning, but overall fulfilling, music career. It's important to form your own definition of success. Being a transgender artist means that there are barriers between you and traditional success. You will eventually come to think this impediment is a good thing, that it frees you from commercial pressure and allows you to experiment without the limitation of trying to sell yourself to the mainstream music industry. Try to not be bitter about any limitations you have. The music industry is like a lottery very few people get tickets to. Make friends with the other people who didn't get tickets either. When you see something that bothers you, try to improve it. Build community, support other musicians and artists. The action of trying will relieve any sense of unfairness that you have.

Believe it or not, you will eventually become a writer, too (like you need *two* careers that your working-class family doesn't consider "work"). After ten years in the music business, you will start writing short stories again. You used to love writing as a child, but eventually trauma took over and you were too dissociative to express yourself in strings of words longer than a couple of verses and a chorus. After five years of therapy, you will be gripped by an urge to write about the past. In this way, I think that I have managed to give you a voice that you don't have in this moment. So, don't worry about being unable to do certain things right now. You will eventually have your say about the situation you are in.

15-year-old Rae, you are trapped in your home, church and school, but let your mind wander to the places you read about in books and get lost in the melodies of songs until it's over. Never forget that it's unjust for people of any gender to be prohibited from doing things they want to do. Use your anger to survive abuse and addiction. Find a good therapist as soon as you can. Continue to rail against sexism (whether you name it right away or not), and encourage others to do the same. Stand up for people. Play guitar solos. Learn computer programs. Assume you can become competent at things. Once you learn how to do any of these things, teach others how to do them. When you finally find someone who loves you and wants to make a home with you, be patient with yourself. Someday you will be sitting in the café you worked at when you were 18, writing a long letter to your teen self, and you'll be texting your word-count updates to your long-term partner and he will text you back, cheering you on.

Most of all, you have all of the right ideas in your current rebellion. The shadows of everything you lived through still cast themselves over you sometimes, but less often. Being queer will always be hard, but you will receive a lot more outside encouragement very soon. You will live to try to encourage other people to make it to a healthy place as well.

Signed,
Rae in their 30s
Montréal

Rae Spoon *is a Montréal-based transgender musician and author. They have toured and performed internationally over the past twelve years. Their book,* First Spring Grass Fire, *is a collection of short stories heavily inspired by coming of age queer in Alberta. Their personal essay,* Femme Cowboy, *can be found in the 2012 Lambda Literary Award-nominated anthology* Persistence. *Rae was long-listed for the Polaris Music Prize in 2008* (superioryouareinferior) *and nominated for two CBC Radio 3 Bucky Awards in 2010. They won the CBC Galaxie Rising Stars award in 2004.*

Victoria B. Robinson

"Yesterday I was clever, so I wanted to change the world. Today I am wise, so I am changing myself."

-Rumi

Dear Victoria,

As a teenager, you can't get away from your family fast enough and don't feel like you want anything to do with them at all. Now, at 31, I take time and money to visit them in Germany from my chosen home in Oakland, California, because I know how important it is to heal these relationships, to forgive and get to a place that allows everyone to fully express themselves. I watch my 4-and-a-half-year-old niece in amazement, as she seems to understand so many things intuitively that I had to learn slowly by going through all these often painful experiences. I watch her dressing up her best male friend—the one she one day wants to marry—in a princess outfit regardless of his protest. And I begin to understand what a strong woman looks like and how much strength and wisdom this little girl has. The strength and wisdom so many girls *would* have if our societies wouldn't feel the need to turn us into nice and cute little beings without demands and voices. This girl is not afraid to use hers, and to do it loudly. She knows what she wants at any given moment, and she has no problem asking for it. There is no doubt in her mind about whether she deserves any of it. Her mere existence should be enough to make people bend over backwards for her. That's what she expects, and that's what she gets. And being nice and cute is only one of the many strategies at her disposal. At 17 you are cocky, and demanding, too. But underneath is this almost unbearable insecurity. When you make demands it is not because you feel worthy, but because you do not. You are constantly fighting. You do not feel loved and protected. You have no idea how beautiful you are, and you are ashamed of almost everything.

I wish you'd already know that you are truly an amazing human being; you always were. I wish you'd already know that life doesn't have to be this hard. And that it won't always be like this. That your natural—and rightful—state is one of happiness, that joy is waiting for you.

I would like to give you a big hug. I would like to embrace you in a way you have never been embraced and assure you that things will be better. You will find the strength in yourself that others tried to suppress. I wish I could tell you that you don't have to fight every single minute of every single day. Some things will just pass with time. Not every battle is yours. There is so much power in stillness. In simply being aware of everything that happens in and outside of yourself.

Eventually you will learn that the home, the sense of belonging you have always yearned for, is not outside yourself. You will not feel at home in Germany, where you were born and raised among your white family members, and you will not feel at home in your father's country either. Not before you have taken care of your wounds. Not before you have taken care of the anger, the pain and all the hurt that has been piled up on top of your amazing, powerful spirit. You will discover your unlimited power: the power to move mountains and move people. The universe is on your side. After exploring all those countries in search of a home and a sense of belonging, you will later be at home wherever you are. And you will know that you are loved. Without having to prove anything. Without needing a big role or title. These will come automatically, but they won't define your worth.

Don't be scared of your power. It is there. All you need to do is make sure to direct it in helpful and constructive ways; helpful to you as well as the rest of the world. Having a positive impact will make you really happy. Causing pain will not. Remember what anger did to you. You wanted someone dead. He died. And now you are wondering whether you are actually responsible. You only did things like that when you felt powerless and violated. You know that this was not your true self. Evil is not true in other people either. Forgive. But keep your distance from those who are destructive and violent. It is not your job to help or heal them. Help and heal yourself. And allow others to help you, too. It's okay to not always be strong. As the Buddhists say: "Pain is a part of life, but suffering is a choice." You do not have to suffer. Make a choice not to. You can make the choice to accept the pain and gain strength out of overcoming it. And you will be so much more powerful as a result.

You are not alone. Never ever.

More often than not, you feel like you have to figure everything out yourself. This is not true. It just seems like it, because you don't have the connections yet. You don't know anything about the Black Germans who have already founded groups and organizations that you will eventually join and become active in. You have come to the conclusion that activism only makes sense if it doesn't kill your spirit, and it must not leave you feeling weak and hurt. You will write about that in a piece called "Shockingly Happy." And later you will learn that many have come to this conclusion before you. That is a good thing. You will read about bell hooks "choosing wellness as an act of resistance," and you will sit close to Alice Walker when she says, "If we are to change anything, we need to have a good time doing it." You will hear Angela Davis recommending that revolutionaries practice yoga. As soon as you realize that you are in very good company, the criticism you get from so-called activists for choosing to take care of yourself and striving for joy will no longer hurt as much.

Speaking of criticism: you will learn not to give a fuck. And that is one of the most important lessons. All the energy and time you spend on trying to please other people, trying to prove yourself, trying to explain yourself... I can tell you one thing: it's not worth it. Eventually you will learn to focus on understanding yourself and expressing yourself authentically. Whether others understand you is not that important. Everyone is crazy. You just have to find people whose craziness is compatible with yours. You will. And they will love and support you all the way.

Speaking of love: it does not make everything better. It makes it easier to bring your wounds to the surface so that you can take care of them. Love is not a game, it is not a competition, and love is certainly not the answer. It's the foundation of a life lived well. The love for every breath and every being on this planet; the love for those who disagree with you and challenge your brain and your heart. Don't direct your love to one person only. Work on loving everybody, beginning with yourself. Sex does not have anything to do with love. Not necessarily. It's an activity that can be deeply spiritual, but at this point in time you haven't even experienced one percent of what is possible. Yes, experiment and explore. Continue to protect yourself. But you should never feel obligated to sleep with anyone. To let someone finish. To follow through because you're supposedly responsible for someone's erection. All this is bullshit, but you haven't learned to stand up for yourself yet. You haven't learned that your boundaries should be respected and that your needs are valid—whether they meet the needs of others or not. Sex is never a solution when you're afraid of losing someone. You don't get love out of a sexual experience, no matter how amazing it is. It's not a compliment when old(er) men are attracted to you, and no matter how often they tell you how mature you are, they are not interested in you because they see you as an equal, but rather because you are a little girl with big breasts and no experience. You will learn this the hard way.

Stop searching. You are already here.

You grew up without knowing your father. If he was mentioned at all, he was the most despicable person on the planet. You always had hope that this wasn't actually true. That he had been looking for you. That finding him would change things. That you would finally feel like you were part of an actual family—a family of people who looked like you and would embrace and appreciate you with everything you were. You always felt estranged in the white family that you grew up in. You left your mom's house on your seventeenth birthday. After years of fighting to be seen, heard and appreciated; years of throwing up in toilets while stuffing the pain deep down inside you. This is when you went searching for your father, for what you imagined was your real family. You always felt like there was a place somewhere out there where you could slow down, where you would feel wanted, where you wouldn't have to prove yourself over and over again.

You will live in various places in Germany, you will move to the United States (east coast then west coast), you will explore Jamaica and cities all over Europe. What keeps you from enjoying them fully is your desire to figure things out, to find absolutes—like an ultimate home. Maybe there is nothing to figure out. Maybe there is no choice to be made. Maybe you can just enjoy wherever you are at any given moment and then move on again. There is no *one* home for you. There is no place that will magically make you feel better. I know now that things won't suddenly change at a certain point in time; change will have to come from within yourself, and you will have to do the work required. After meeting your father this year, it will take you ten years to truly forgive him. And that is okay. You will get to a place with him that is not controlled by anger and pain, and it will be wonderful. One day it will not feel fake when he writes, "I love you" at the end of a letter. You will write the same thing and it will be true. You will be able to love the people who did what they were able to do at any given time. You will realize that holding on to anger does not do anything for you—at least nothing positive. Your willingness to forgive will help others do the same. To forgive each other and themselves. This is an amazing contribution you will make to the world. Be proud of coming so far. Be proud of overcoming that which holds you hostage. Be proud of being aware that you are by no means finished, that you will continue to make mistakes, to hurt people who don't deserve it, to hurt yourself because you feel guilty. There is no such thing as perfection. It's all a process, and what you have is this specific moment. Nothing more, nothing less. Make it special, make it magical, and do something nice for yourself and everyone around you.

There are no right or wrong choices. Experiment!

You are stressed out all the time because you are so convinced that you a) have to make a choice, and b) should be making the right one. I wish you would be able to relax a little bit. You will not find out what *your* career and purpose is. I still haven't figured it out. After working in the academic field, as a journalist, a TV producer, a PR and marketing manager, a group fitness instructor, an empowerment coach, a translator, an event planner, a moderator, a book publisher, a non-profit worker and being many other things, you will still not know what the one thing is. And what does that pressure do for you? You have many talents, passions and interests. Why not use all of them? Not at the same time, like when instead of choosing one or two you played six different instruments and finally gave up all of them because you were so exhausted. Do it consecutively. You will get to experience all of these things and many more, and you will learn to focus on one or two areas at a time. You will make plans and agreements with yourself. This way you fully know why you are doing something and for what period of time. Like right now. I allow myself to live in phases. In this phase I am working full-time. This doesn't mean I'm not a writer anymore, and this doesn't mean I'm not an activist. It only means that I focus on other things for a while, and I am aware of the reasons for this choice. Life is not so serious after all. Things change all the time. Whenever you think that you are an adult, I would like to remind you of one thing: you are not! Growing up takes time. This we don't learn until we're much older, until we know that we are never done, we are never at the point where we can say, I know who I am and what I believe: I am now an adult. This will not happen.

Because we evolve until the day we die. Possibly even longer.

Choose your fights! Not every struggle is yours.

Yes, you are a compassionate person. That is a good thing! You bring home stray animals to rescue and nurture, you protect the fat kids from the bullies, you join every group and initiative, you volunteer at an animal shelter, and you start your own clubs left and right whenever you feel like something has to be done. All of this is very noble. But it is neither effective nor is it fun. You tend to get caught up in all these projects, and in the end you don't do them justice, because you're just so tired. And hurt, because you can never fulfill your expectations. There is no gratitude for those that are running around trying to save the world; it's quite the opposite, as you know. The key is not to get involved in everything and tire yourself out. The key is to choose a very small number of issues that a) are very close to your heart, and b) which you can have the most meaningful effect on. Why not try picking something that comes easily to you?

Growing up, you always had to fight—against injustice, against prejudice, against the devaluation you experienced because you were a girl and even more so because you were Black. Or merely, you had to fight because people around you were so darn ignorant. These battles were not those that could have healed you, but they kept you busy, absorbing all your energies and leaving you behind like an empty shell. Hard and fragile at the same time. Offering protection to others while not being tough enough to save yourself. Nobody prepared you for the racist incidents you encountered. You never felt like someone was protecting you. You didn't even know anything about being Black then. You had no idea what it meant, as everybody else was white. There were no words for who you were, and the names that people gave you were painful.

All you knew is that you were wrong, that you had to constantly prove your abilities and how nice you were, how well you were able to speak your mother tongue. You tried to kill yourself. Because your eyes never turned blue, your hair never turned blond and your body never was shaped the way that was supposedly right and attractive. You wasted so many years and didn't even realize that there were actually people who loved you. They were right there.

In these moments of doubt and desperation, I want you to know what you will grow into: a powerful, strong woman with a circle of wonderful, supportive friends all over the world. A woman whose voice is heard and appreciated. A woman who doesn't feel the need to explain herself and apologize for her feelings all the time. A woman with an edge. A woman who knows that she has to focus in order to achieve something.

Something? No, in fact you will achieve anything—anything you ever wanted and more. That's what you'll expect, and that is what you'll get.

Victoria B. Robinson is a Black German activist, poet, author, academic, empowerment and creativity coach and curator. She has published four books, and her writing, which often deals with her experiences with racism in Germany, has been published in a number of books, anthologies, magazines and performed on stages. She contributed to the exhibition "Homestory Deutschland: Black Biographies in History and the Present," which has been touring through Europe and the African continent. Victoria is a founding member of the Black European Women's Council and Oakland Ink, and the founder of ISD SiSTARS, a German Black women's initiative.

Kit Wilson-Yang

Dear Chris,

I want to tell you a story. It's a story about patterns.

Three years ago for you, many more for myself, the middle school in our town was still open. Kids at that school came from all over town, some from the farming communities outside. By a cruel stroke of some distant pen, all the kids in the school were at an age that many people start the long, hard, life-changing experience we call puberty. Like most important things in life, the state is real cold about showing you how to deal with it. The school was full of rumours and rooms that people had long forgotten the purpose of. Behind doors that students never saw open were tales of grisly demise, lost virginity, ghosts, pot smoke so thick you couldn't see the ghosts, and the room that all the teachers drank in. You went there in grade seven, some of the kids had been there since grade six and you would only stay until eighth grade. It was the only school in that area of town, tucked under the escarpment, at once captured and fortified by the cliffs. It was the oldest school in town, so old it still had boys' and girls' entrances. There was a stream that ran along the school behind a fence, and when you first arrived there you felt like you'd been dropped off on the set of a New England horror film. The teachers were either far too eager to meet the new students or wore scowls of extreme disapproval.

Even before you got to the school it was terrifying. People talked about the *grub table* where you would end up if you wore the same pair of pants two days in a row. Once on the table, the entire school would spit on you for being so gross. You couldn't wear sweatpants because someone would pull your pants down when you had your back turned at your locker. You couldn't have your back turned at your locker because someone would give you a wedgie. You should wear boxer shorts, not briefs. People might think you're gay. So much fear going into that school, eh? You remember. You'll always remember. You self-policed yourself so intensely that first year of middle school. But a year ago, when you started high school and you actually did get a welcome worthy of a bad, white, suburban high school teen movie, you weren't nearly as scared. There had been no *grub table*, and there you did not get one wedgie nor did you see one dished out. You thought the rumours of grade nines being forced to push pennies with their noses and getting their asses paddled were just that: rumours. They sure did have a paddle. And they sure did have pennies they wanted pushed. "Boys will be boys," someone will say. Your friend who got paddled the hardest transferred schools right away, and you never heard about him again. I ran into his brother a few years ago; he joined the Israeli Army. The one punk that went to your school, the kid with the best mohawk you'll ever see, got beat up so badly he transferred before you even got there. Kids keeping other kids in line: what a lesson in social control! Little wonder you've got the secrets you do. Don't worry, no judgment here.

That middle school, haunted by the rumours of hundreds of nervous kids playing out their insecurities on each other like creeks blaming streams for flowing, had a paved playground with some rusted, broken basketball nets and chipped yellow paint outlines of games with shifting rules. But no one played those games because they were too cool. Every lunch hour you would stand with your friend in the middle of the pavement and look past the chain link fence keeping the students off the escarpment and away from the creek, counting the train cars as the freight rolled by. Sometimes there were more than a hundred of them. Sometimes the two of you would tell each other numbers, as if you were at the centre of a clock face, to locate people you thought looked funny. One day you were doing that and some older kids yelled at you, "Hey freak! Are you a boy or a girl?!" and you yelled back, "What do you think?!" One of the kids replied, "I dunno. That's why I asked." He wasn't yelling when he said it. You were furious! You had just bought a girls' shirt with Mom because the sale clerk figured you for a girl, and not long before that your relatives in Australia sent you a doll in a yellow dress for your birthday because they figured you for a girl as well. Never mind the fights about long hair versus boys' hair and that business with the tutu at the sitter's so many years ago. Of course you were furious. You had been making fun of other people, albeit with a bit more discretion than your critics, and you yourself were singled out as a weirdo. You were trying very hard to be what you understood yourself to be: a boy. And those kids were missing all the cues. Or maybe picking up on all the cues...

Either way, two things happened that day: you were publicly made fun of for your ambiguous gender, and you made yourself feel better by putting down other people. A classic tactic you'll see lots of other people employ, I promise. Teachers, students, parents, police and relatives. That day it made you feel okay, but watching other people do it, Chris, you're gonna hate it.

You walk home from school every day with the same bunch of kids, a mix of boys and girls. You all stop at the same convenience store each day, some of you stealing penny candy that costs a nickel, and some of you buying it. The boys hit and throw things at the girls they think are cute. Some push them into bushes or snow banks. Maybe they just make fun of them. The girls you like hit them back. You don't hit the girls you walk home with. Back in grade school you tried it, and when you kicked Julia, she was pissed. And hurt. She did not want to play with you and you felt like a jerk. You were. Lucky for you, Julia was clear with her reaction; she taught you that it sucks to hurt someone you care about, that it doesn't show that you care about them. They get hurt, and you're a jerk for it. Unlucky for Julia, your lesson was her getting kicked. This is the first time you encounter this kind of pattern. So in eighth grade, with your long curly hair, trench coat and Nine Inch Nails shirt, you don't hit the people you have crushes on. Your friends do.

That year, you did that school project on anarchy for your English class. Hooray for the teacher that let you do that! Remember those books you took out from the library you couldn't read because the words were longer than all of your names combined? And that one book on Sacco and Vanzetti that you read? That book was great! How crummy was that—those two men getting blamed and killed for a crime they didn't commit because they were Italian and part of a political movement that threatened the state? Good for you for noticing the injustice. The focus of your presentation on garbage collection in a hypothetical anarchist state was clever, but perhaps not the most enticing way to introduce your peers to the idea that they didn't need a boss or the cops. There was a comic you printed off the Internet; it had a picture of a boss yelling at a worker, who goes home and yells at his wife, who then yells at her child, who then kicks a cat. Remember? It made you think of Dad coming home from work angry with his day, and his dad coming home from his work angry with his day. In a few years you'll see that comic as an oversimplification of a really important idea. But right then, reading that comic, watching Dad come home from work and unload his shitty day on the household, you hold your cat real tight, committing yourself to never kick her, no matter how bad your day is.

Then you have Miss Bedford for a homeroom teacher. She wears collared shirts and vests and smokes heavily. You've been dabbling in the habit yourself, but it just makes you incredibly dizzy in a way that is fun at first, but later makes you nauseous. You have to sneak off school property at lunch to do it. Because you are explicitly breaking a rule, it feels amazing. Miss Bedford was your grade seven science teacher and you thought she was the meanest thing around. But that year she was different: she was friendlier, slower than the year before, more patient. Her partner died that year. They had been together for decades and never married. You realize you don't know anything about Miss Bedford. She looks so worn out after years of teaching bratty rich kids, getting made fun of for her size and her smoking. The class didn't even know she had a lover. She is suddenly so human to you it feels impossible. You watch her sit on the stool in front of the class and crumple, tears streaming from her eyes. She doesn't make a sound. She looks like she's lived lives longer than you can perceive. You watch her and wonder: *Where will she go after school today? Did her lover live with her? Is her house empty? Does she have kids?* For the first time, you realize that the people around you have things going on in their lives you have no idea about.

This is the year you got on the principal's honour roll. I know the assembly is fresh in your mind. You're sitting with your class in the gym, all the classes lined up like platoons facing the stage. You go up with the rest of the kids who excelled academically that year. And none of your friends are there. At first you're surprised, then you look at the line up of kids. You recognize them from other extracurriculars, you never see them in the smoking area, you know where they live and you know their parents. The longer you look at who is in line to get a little plaque from the principal and who isn't you see a stark pattern. None of the kids who hang out in the parking lot selling or smoking weed, none of the kids you know that have something at home other than piano lessons, homework, two parents and lunches made for them, are in line. The only kids in line for the honour roll are folks with stable homes and money. The only people that stand out to you in the line are the two other Asian kids in your grade. The absence of your friends is your first real lesson in class dynamics. That absence hits like a fist in the gut. You went home and smashed the plaque on your bedroom floor.

You're seeing all these little patterns: people not knowing how to express that they care for one another, people being so much more than what you see, how others do not see you as you see yourself, the way other people take out their anger on people they feel they have power over when they themselves feel powerless, cycles of abuse from work to family or from family to family, your lesson from Julia coming entirely at her expense. There are huge ideas swirling around you. These patterns are still playing themselves out. How many times are you put in a position to explain your race, or asked to teach people about what being Chinese is, when you haven't the slightest idea? You grew up with white people. But there you are, being asked to teach people who make fun of you for being mixed. You're seeing patterns: the gym teacher asking Dan to tell the whole class about the blow job his girlfriend gave him in the park at lunch, boys guilting the girls around them into different sex acts, girls shaming other girls for the way they look and your friend who says he just "likes the aesthetic of being gay" but is really not gay (who could blame him with those paddle-happy jocks around?). One of two Black kids at school breaks down and the other disappears. Suburban depressions and family abuses. Friends get kicked out of their houses. All that weird Zionist propaganda stapled to all the telephone poles in the neighbourhood. Teachers hating on some kids way more than others. Girls that look too "trashy" getting picked on and kicked out by teachers who feel threatened by femininity and sexuality. You aren't imagining all of these actions playing out around you that you notice and find yourself reacting to. You see it.

Keep on noticing these patterns! Trust your reactions! People are telling you about all kinds of discrimination every day in the way they describe their interactions with each other. And the more you listen and watch, the more you're gonna listen and watch yourself. What are you saying and how are you saying it? What are you doing and how are you doing it?

You are going to make some awful mistakes, and the people who get mad at you for them are going to be wonderful teachers to you. That process is going to hurt a whole bunch. But fear not! They'll be lessons you're glad to learn. Like the lesson you learned kicking Julia Greenberg in the shin.

It's never going to hurt any less, you're just going to get used to it. I don't want to lie and tell you it's going to get better, but you'll manage, you're so much stronger than you think—I promise!

You are isolated, unable to name the things you are, the urges you have. Even with the Internet, you wouldn't know what to look for. But you know the clothes you like wearing, and you know how good they make you feel. You know the desires you have and the things that turn you on. As hard as it is not to fear them and what the world would do if you expressed them, trust those desires. They are true feelings and you aren't the only one who has them. It's not going to get easier out of high school, but it is going to be more honest. The relief of not hiding will be tremendous.

I want to give you a life without expectations. Expectations weigh so heavily on us. There are appearances to keep up. People expect you to grow up into a good example of a man. They expect a marriage; a decent job; safe, left-leaning liberal politics and a commitment to non-violence. People expect you to become all the things they've trained you to be, things they will not or can not name. They expect you to uphold social codes they themselves don't even believe exist anymore. Sexism moves like a glacier, changing the landscape so you can never comment on a beautiful tree, a lovely stream or staggering embankment without referencing the glacier that froze the land and stripped the soil. And that water is still here, pulling the earth, slowly stealing stones, weathering them and leaving only sand. But this glacier isn't natural. People made it, and I believe, as you do, that people can unmake it. I want to give you a life without expectations so you can grow in all the directions you can imagine. So you can flourish.

You're going to get out of that town and find the words for what you are. There's a line I read a while back that I really loved: "I promise not to lie, or require anyone else to lie."* So much is going to change! I'm not in a place where I can tell the truth all the time, but someday, I hope we both are.

I suppose that's a few stories. There are so many to tell, wouldn't you agree?

xo
Kit

*Dorthy Allison from "Public Silence, Private Terror" published in *Skin*.

———————————————

Kit Wilson-Yang *is a Toronto-based musician, writer and artist, who creates work about colonization, heartbreak, friendship and being a transwoman in the world. Her most recent zine,* ancient land, new water, *is a collection of stories and poems about her personal experiences of transition.* interyang.blogspot.com.

Rozena Maart

April 15th, 1978

Dear Rozena,

Happy birthday! How wonderful it must be to be 16 years old. Two more years of school and then it is off to university, as you've recently indicated to your guidance teacher at school. You will be the first in your family to attend, and this in itself marks a big step in how far the country has come from the days when Black, Coloured and Indian girls were not allowed to go to school.

Birthdays are always great to celebrate with friends and family: they are an opportunity to bring people together. However awkward and difficult, Rozena, there will be a time when you *will* meet your father, though perhaps not this year. At 18 you will have the ability to travel and visit him in East London; it is a twelve hour drive from Cape Town along the eastern coast. You'll be able to get a driver's license by then, and once you've finished school and you're in attendance at university, you'll be in a better position to face him, address the issue with your mother and find out for yourself what really happened between them. All young girls go through periods of wanting to know where they come from—it is only natural to want to know more about your absent father and about your heritage. Looking around the room at family gatherings to see who you look like might be a thing of the past when you meet him.

Your teacher, Stella Clark, was able to support you through this and she has become quite an important part of your life. Take her advice: don't let your father's absence become the focus of your life. You've done well without him thus far and you will continue to do without him—your writing reveals this already at your age.

Keep up the writing, and keep up the drama training at the Space Theatre on Long Street on Saturday afternoons. Young women need to have forums that allow them the kind of expression that you are known for. Theatre is a joy and will give you the possibility of bringing the lived experience to the stage in very particular ways. In theatre, especially within the improvisation sessions that Colin facilitates, you are able to act out a fear or anxiety and can allow for the emotion to be reflected to others in your group. The feedback session offers input from others, and it is here where you see yourself go through the different stages of tackling these fears. In this way, you learn what your responses might be when confronted with a situation yourself because you have your whole group there—people who know you and care about you. This is the joy of theatre: it is a place where your emotions are displayed, channeled through different routes, poured into different characters; and it is a place where you learn to build and to unpeel characters.

Drama and performance—both of which will play a big role in your fiction writing one day—are necessary. You have much to offer. The street theatre you organized in Lavender Hill was important— even if people laughed. There are those who laugh because crying is too painful. At least you are able to raise awareness of rape and sexual abuse. 16-year-olds in South Africa live in a world not so different from the rest of the world. Anti-apartheid organizations will have to take rape and sexual assault on-board; women make up half the population, and if this happens to women around the world, then surely it must be taken up in political organizations. I think you are right in insisting that your youth group has discussion sessions on rape. As Mamma says all the time: if it matters to women, it matters to the world. Even from a woman who did not go to high school or university, you will learn just how meaningful Mamma's words are. She would have loved to go but her generation of girls was not allowed. This means that you have to value your education even more. We do not come into the world like fully baked cakes; someone has provided the ingredients before us—several men and women—and it is up to us to honour their memory and to honour the history of how we came to be educated. Your generation has been buttered in the hands of our grandmothers, who made sure that our lives would be greater than theirs—always remember that. We are all as great as the community of women who raised us, and nothing is greater than the gift of gratitude.

There is an amazing group of young people among you, and even the boys within the group know this. I am so proud of your determination to bring this to the attention of a youth group that is coordinated by men and women from the United Democratic Front (UDF), even if we know that the African National Congress is banned in the country and their objectives are directed through the UDF. How many people your age can say that they have lived through what you have? This is only the beginning. I am glad that you're having a traditional Sweet Sixteen party, even if it is not quite as traditional as everyone else's. I am certainly very pleased to see that you are embracing this year with greater optimism. Last year was difficult: no one could have predicted the effect of Steve Biko's murder on the nation. You have those pamphlets with you—the ones that have been distributed around the country by Black Consciousness revolutionaries. Continue to read them. You know where to keep banned readings—in the plastic bottom drawer of the fridge, with all the starchy vegetables. You will come to rely on Steve Biko's words as you grow older; their meaning will grow as your body grows, as experience grows, as human life expands.

Each year you will find deeper meaning in the words of a man who brought your nation a wealth of knowledge, who was able to situate the mind within the body of the oppressed like no one else because he was able to engage us in our role in the apartheid process and in the process of decolonization. He taught us to look inward; that consciousness is pain, it is not something someone hands you as a gift. The gift itself is the possibility of self-interrogation and self-examination, with the tools of analysis Biko left you.

Many young people of your age were left speechless by his death—but the struggle continues. For Steve Biko, like for Malcolm X, it was a choice between freedom and death.

South Africa still has a long way to go when it comes to freedom, but we will get there. The road towards freedom means the commitment to not allow your being to be defined by a regime set on educating the Black population toward inferiority. When you return from the protest march, like you've done in the past two years, return to your books. A solid education, despite the odds against young people, means the possibility of a great future. You will have to be ready and equipped to live in a post-apartheid society; it will happen, so don't give up now. The police killed Biko—don't let anybody kill the spirit that has been ignited.

As for your first women's group at your school and most likely the first in the country—how wonderful! March 1978 is a good month to have started. How wonderful that Biko inspired this in all of you.

There is no shame in calling yourself a feminist, even at your age. Wendy and Ayesha and you—three people are enough for a woman's group to meet and organize discussions at school. One can only start with your friends, especially if they are the people who come from the same background as you.

The start of the Rape Crisis organization in the country is a huge milestone, even if it is composed of white women at this stage—it will not always be that way. Even at this stage, your presence means that rape and sexual assault will have to be on the agenda in every political organization. You will meet Anne Mayne, but know that she is no push-over; she is a woman of substance and determination. Any woman who makes it public that she was gang-raped, starts an organization with the help of a handful of friends and travels half-way around the world to meet other women who have founded rape crisis organizations means business. Since she has replied to your letter, ask her about doing a talk at your school.

It has been almost three years since the forced removal from District Six. Mamma did not think that you could cope with school. She herself has to try so hard now that Pappa has had both his legs amputated. There is sorrow in the lives of many grandparents who have had their lives cut and sliced by legislation that has attempted to dehumanize them, but look how Mamma and Pappa wake up every morning. Look at how they still continue with their day, and how they still see their friends and still have parties. The move from District Six, referred to as the old slave quarter, was the removal from their home—despite how it has been written about in the newspapers. It was your home, not only your place of birth, and someday it will be your home again. It is where Mamma has lived all her life, and where Pappa has lived since he was 18 years old. Pappa's family is from the Eastern Cape, and Mamma has Javanese ancestry on account of the British and Dutch voyages of exploitation, usurpation and extraction, which led to enslavement of each of their ancestors. Their last names provide evidence of their enslavement under Dutch rule—Maart and September. This is the world that you were born into, and it is the world from which you will grow. You are only a slave if you allow your enslaved history to keep you shackled to a reality that situates your past as present. Mamma and Pappa know that all too well. As grandparents, they have made sure that all of their grandchildren know their history; there is good reason for that. Without knowledge of our history, we are not able to live in the present. Being able to know—like you do—is a gift. Your grandparents, who tell stories at bedtime, are your historians; and you will reflect on this as you grow older.

The stories you hear from Mamma and her brother Boeta are not the kind you'll find in history books. Boeta fought in the Second World War. Officially he, like all of the Indian and Black men, was not allowed to carry ammunition because there was a fear that they might turn it on their oppressors. And yet, he went. He went because he was rounded up—picked out by men in police cars who drove around District Six and looked for tall, handsome men who were strong-boned and well-built. Boeta, like all the Black and Indian men, got a bicycle upon his return. I know that he jokes about it, but do not let those jokes fool you. He has no regrets, as he says all the time, but deep down inside, he and his generation thought that their participation would make a difference. He has said many a time that he hopes it makes a difference to girls like you—girls who know just how much they risked, who will not treat them as ignorant old fools who trusted their racist oppressors. They knew their realties. They knew! They knew their realities, and still they participated in a war that they were drafted to, with the belief that they would be seen as men, as human, as people with the same belief in nationalism as their white counterparts.

And now to something a little more delicate: your hives. You started getting them on August 4th—the day that the family and most of the De Villiers Street residents from District Six were forcibly removed. You've had them for two years in a row, and you will continue to get them until you are able to draw connections between the silence that surrounds the forced removal of thousands of us and your body's reaction. Your body breaks the silence by pushing hives to the surface of your skin on the same day each year. This is not a matter of shame but of pain. You will learn that our bodies carry our histories, that dates and times lie buried within us, beneath the surface. And they will surface again to remind you never to forget what happened to our people.

Your painful history is resting in your body. It will stay hidden until you are ready to reveal it to yourself. When you are ready to face it, to pick what has bonded to your flesh, written itself in your blood, attached itself to your nerve endings, you will find your own way. We each have our own way to track and trace memories— they are always there, they never go away—but they wait, softly and silently, until we are ready to speak. One day your hives will speak, and when they do, listen to them.

Your mother has a way of understanding what Mamma and Pappa are able to hear. When she tells you not to talk about District Six to them, it is because she does not want them to feel as though they let you down. They fought hard, but in the end the government won. When Pappa stares out the window for hours on end, with one portion of his trousers folded and clipped under where his flesh used to be, he is thinking of the days when he was a fisherman. That was his trade; it is one his father taught him, and his father to his son. Pappa, and his father too, always had that sense that the sea was something that could not be taken away from them. Then when Irvin and Johnson regulated the sea and banned fishermen from catching their daily supply for their community, it destroyed a part of their hearts. He will sit and stare at the sea for hours to have that connection again. And now, with the move to Lavender Hill, this is more difficult because he can only see the mountain. Remember when he used to take all of us fishing? Remember how we learnt to thread a fishing rod and know where to find bait? You will never forget those days. When you see him staring through the window on a rainy day, go to him and tell him how much you appreciate them.

I just want to say this to you: don't give up your poetry for anyone. The fight for freedom cannot be done without poetry. We need words that curl around our tongues, that make us feel things, that allow us to sink into ourselves, that urge us toward greater places within the world. Poetry is our bread; butter it with pleasure.

And now for some parting words:
Never lose your smile and your laughter, not even your whistle.

Love and kisses.
Your 50-year-old self.

Rozena Maart *is a professor of Gender Studies and Director at the Centre for Critical Research on Race and Identity at the University of Kwa Zulua Natal in Durban, South Africa. Born in District Six, Cape Town, she was nominated for the "Woman of the Year" award at age 24 for her work in the area of violence against women and for co-founding the first Black feminist organization in South Africa, Women Against Repression [W.A.R.]. Rozena has published several journal articles and essays and three books, including the award-winning* Rosa's District Six *and* The Writing Circle.

Elisha Lim

Dear 14-year-old Elisha,

I'm going to tell you something depressing—but wait, then I'm going to tell you something beautiful. I'm telling you this because I love you.

Okay, so right now someone is always telling you what to do. Right? All your life, your parents decided your schools, your schools decided your uniform; even your extracurricular activities were researched and paid for by the adults around you. Your choices have been basically Yes or No. Do you want to take Speech and Drama? Yes or No?

Things will change. And it'll be fun, but it'll also have a lot of disadvantages. Your family will move to North America, and they will leave you there. Your dad will leave first. He will take your sister with him back to Singapore, and she will take her clothes and her music and her habits and all of her familiar things. Your mum will leave last, in a taxi outside the front door. It's one of the weirdest moments in your life.

And then it's over and you're alone, for good. Suddenly you're in charge of everything. This is why I need to talk to you. I'm shouting to you as loud as I can and I want you to hear me.

You're in charge. Life is up to you. But you don't realize it yet. You keep waiting for instructions, because that's what you've always done. You're on a kind of obedient auto-pilot. You get sick and you wait for someone to look after you or to tell you what to do. But no one does, and you end up hailing a taxi to the hospital by yourself, feeling kind of shocked. Christmas comes and you wait for decorations to go up and presents to appear and somebody to just tell you what to do. But they don't, and you end up very lonely walking around a ghost of a city.

Wonderful things pass by all around you, like zine fairs and Mandarin classes and art school and gallery volunteering and Queer parties; and nobody tells you to go to them. So you don't. Instead you take university classes that don't inspire you. You get a degree that you don't care about. And you follow your friends into boring, destructive frat parties that, truthfully, suck.

Okay. So this is the beautiful thing I want to tell you: somewhere inside of you, you know what you want. You know what you long for, and you know that you can make it come true.

You want to go to art school. I know that. You want to so much that it hurts—it hurts with the fear of disobedience, because it's not what your parents recommend. It hurts with the fear that you'll fail. But it's okay, you can do it. If you want to, you have to try. Start looking at art schools online. Don't worry about getting in, just see what they ask for. Let the seeds plant in your mind.

You want to live in New York. You can do that, too! Look at schools there and see if they offer scholarships. I know you're only 14, but I just want you to dream and to think about how to make your dreams come true all by yourself.

You want to get to know your grandma better. Your parents won't realize it, but you can say so. You can go to her house on Sundays and help her cook or make flower arrangements. You can take the bus on your own—it's the only way you'll get there.

I want to help you skip all those lonely years. I want you to stop waiting for instructions. I want you to figure out what you want—and go out and get it by yourself.

But being in charge takes practice. So I've made you an exercise. This is an exercise in naming your dreams. Fill it out with the wildest, most incredible honesty. I've put in some of my own suggestions to get the ball rolling. Some of your answers will change with time, but that's okay. For now, you can start to find the steps to do them. Baby steps are great. Figure out what you want, and then figure out how to get it.

Don't worry if people say you can't want these things. Don't forget: you're in charge.

I love you.
Elisha, aged 33

<u>I want to live in these cities</u>
1. New York
2.
3.
Steps I have to take:
1.
2.
3.
4.
5.

<u>I want to try these jobs</u>
1. Celebrity makeup artist
2.
3.
Steps I have to take:
1.
2.
3.
4.
5.

<u>I want to learn these skills</u>
1.
2.
3.

Steps I have to take:

1.

2.

3.

4.

5.

I want to speak these languages

1.

2.

3.

Steps I have to take:

1.

2.

3.

4.

5.

I want to pursue these careers

1.

2.

3.

Steps I have to take:

1.

2.

3.

4.

5.

I want to learn these instruments

1.

2.

3.

Steps I have to take:

1.

2.

3.

4.

5.

<u>I want to live in these homes</u>

1.

2.

3.

Steps I have to take:

1.

2.

3.

4.

5.

<u>I want to affect these changes</u>

1.

2.

3.

Steps I have to take:

1.

2.

3.

4.

5.

<u>I want to learn these recipes</u>

1.

2.

3.

Steps I have to take:

1.

2.

3.

4.

5.

<u>I want to meet these people</u>

1.

2.

3.

Steps I have to take:

1.

2.

3.

4.

5.

<u>I want to have these adventures</u>

1.

2.

3.

Steps I have to take:

1.

2.

3.

4.
5.

Elisha Lim *is an artist and activist who demands radical change and anti-oppressive justice. Their comics have been acclaimed by Alison Bechdel and Shary Boyle and their films circulate LGBTQ film festivals around the world, but their proudest accomplishments have been group efforts: like making* Xtra! Canada's Gay and Lesbian Newspaper *adopt gender neutral pronouns and directing Montréal's first racialized pride week.*

Lee Maracle

Dear Lee,

I can see you sitting on the shore of Howe Sound, our water's edge, home of the giant octopus and the deepest sound in North America. I know what you are doing there. I want to say something to you, but it is not possible. I am you. I am 62, but right now you don't intend to live that long. In fact, you intend this to be your last day here on earth. You are already a planner. You planned this out very carefully and with some not-bad logic, but it will end comically—not that that will make you feel good. You will have a breakdown—*meltdown* everyone today calls it—but you will recover. You won't feel like you will recover for a very long time, but you will. Your recovery will be painful and somewhat abortive, by that I mean you will climb out of this dark emotional and spiritual abyss that you have fallen into, fall back into it and climb out again—several times. You will live for a time knowing that you are at the edge of this abyss before you realize you are never going back there.

It is a Saturday night and the dark is deep. The moon is hidden by clouds more or less chronically in this part of the world—British Columbia is a rainforest after all. You love this moon when it finds its way through the cloud cover, but you have no idea why. You are so focused on the fact that white people don't like you, and because you are surrounded and tormented by them, day in and day out, you can't seem to sit and explore what you love. You have been in school now for eleven years, and the moments that were not spent being beaten by other children, who were validated by teachers, were spent being alone and lonely. You cannot admit it right now, but you want oneness with them, despite how they feel about you. You can't possibly know that wanting oneness is both natural and cultural. The long hours spent at school away from those who love you have crippled your spirit just a little; they hunch your spine; they pain you physically and emotionally. That is sad, but they have not harmed your intellect.

Right now you know enough to see what is wrong with the world, but you don't have any experience at bucking the tide, pushing back on the wrongs and winning small battles day by day. In short, you think you know and understand the world, but you don't. No one can understand the world outside of their own agency in transforming and affecting it. We can only understand the world in our tenacious struggle to engage and change it. You do not intend to give yourself that opportunity. Of course, you don't see it that way.

"Nothing is ever going to change." This is how you see it. Your conscious experience is true. So far, nothing has changed. Not one effort of yours to stop the bullying, stop the sexual attacks, stop the hatred, has produced a positive result. It is fair for you to say nothing will ever change, it is also untrue. "Reality is always false"; the very moment we get a grip on reality, it begins to transform. The transformation required is a social one, not a personal one. In order for the violence to end, others—non-natives—need to join the struggle to end it, and right now no one besides the violated seems to know or be able to accept that it is going on.

You are young. This is the most beautiful time of your life, but the world sees you as ugly. They remind you every day: "Ugly *cleutch*, ugly squaw, ugly Indian." Others do not dare to be your friend for fear of what others might think of them: "Injun lover." Your family doesn't hear you in a way that helps. "I can't continue going to school with these people, it is killing me." "Don't listen to them." It is hard not to hear a thousand people whispering, yelling or speaking in your face. I know you don't believe them. You have never accepted the "stupid" or "ugly" monikers proffered on you, but you want it to stop. You want friendship from someone at that school. The one friend you had moved and now there is no one left—at least it feels that way.

I do want you to listen to your detractors, hear them and wonder how they got to be how they are. Never forget them. Remember what they are saying. Take care to mark how many of them actually say it. Get petty and actually count them—it isn't a thousand. Come on, you know it isn't all of them, it isn't even most of them. Problem is, this makes no difference to you at this moment. First, it is enough of them, and second, the rest of them retreat afraid. That is not how you see it though, you see them as cowards. The majority give the minority permission to make your life a living hell and no human being signs up for that, so I sympathize. You can't possibly know that it isn't cowardice. Those who don't like how you are treated suffer from the same dilemma you have: they know enough to see something is wrong, but not enough to change it. So you have decided to return to the spirit world. I know you are not going to succeed at this.

You thought that if you brought your winter coat, put on your boots, donned a good wool sweater and paddled out into the sound in a leaky skiff on a night covered in deep blue-black, you could drown yourself. It made so much sense. After all, you can't swim very well; I still can't. The water is cold. It is deep. The skiff is leaky. And all these clothes when wet will weigh so much more than you do. How could you know that the coat was waterproof and, at the moment of truth, you would be out there in that sound bobbing like a big balloon, thinking, "Oh fuck, this is embarrassing." That comedy that you resented so much in your family will save you.

You aren't through with tragedy. After you leave school you will also leave home and bring tragedy down upon yourself; "If the state won't kill us, we will have to kill ourselves" will be your mantra for a while. But then, one day in California, you will be watching television, drowning in your own despair, and Coretta King will hand you a key—a key that will continue to open doors for you. Even today, this key opens doors for me. "We are going to bring love back to our community." Agency, bring love back to our community, activism. She meant Black people, but you knew these words were for you.

As I look at you at the water's edge, I chuckle. There have been some great changes in my lifetime, and at the same time, quite a lot of not-a-whit-sort-of-non-changing. The "same ol' same ol'" of colonial racism lingers on the Canadian horizon. I hate to tell you, but we are still colonized, there is still so much racist murder of Indigenous women going on. But there are people all over the world who want something more for us now—make no mistake, it is not the majority, but there are enough people out there rooting for us that it makes me weep tears of joy. The thing that is going to be different for you is that one day, you will pack up a bag of *shtwehn,* some of that half-breed *pemmican* and push back on the world.

You will find a tiny group of six people who have moved past "knowing enough of what's wrong" to knowing how to change it. This group will have the audacity to call itself Red Power. This is what you will fall in love with. They have the cheek and brass to demonstrate against the church for abusing children at Residential School in 1968—all six of them. You will fall in love with this, too. You will find your own fearlessness along with them, and even though you won't win as many battles as you fight, you will be happy taking up the standard over and over and insisting on being a free agent. You will also learn to differentiate between struggling for something and struggling against something. You will learn when to resist oppression and when to accept others as they are. You will learn that the first transformation has to occur inside of you. You will fall in love with the sense of justice buried deeply underneath your anger, resentment and despair. You will learn that it is your anger that drives you to the edge of the abyss and that the lack of belief in other people's ability to change is hooked to your own unwillingness to look inside and transform. When that first moment of self-reflection leads you to transform, you will be inspired, move away from the edge of suicide and never go back.

You will stumble upon a group of women throwing pies in the faces of politicians at about the same time you wake and realize you are a woman. As such, you will learn that you have put up with the greater weight of colonization and racism and that these two phenomena manifest in your communities as patriarchy. Through these women you will find agency inside of yourself as a feminist. This will help you to find allies among other feminists. They will not be very good allies in the beginning, but then, you won't be so good as an ally either. At first, you will see them as "do-gooders" who are trying to use their privilege to "help" the Indians, but when you realize you cannot speak for them in the same way they cannot speak for you, things will begin to change. It will take time, struggle, and thoughtful and not-so-thoughtful discussions— fights even—but eventually common allegiances will inspire you, and the world will seem a much more hopeful place than it does now.

In the meantime, flip your little flippers, get to shore and rest; enjoy the comic end to this suicide attempt. Commit to living here on earth for the long haul. It gets better.

Lee Maracle is an award-winning author and instructor, gifted orator, mother, grandmother and a member of the Sto: Loh nation. She has spent much of her time doing healing and cultural reclamation work in Aboriginal communities across Canada. She is the author of the critically-acclaimed Sojourner's *and* Sundogs, Ravensong, Bobbi Lee, Daughters Are Forever, Will's Garden, Bent Box *and* I Am Woman, *and co-editor of a number of anthologies, including* My Home As I

Remember *and* Telling It: Women and Language across Culture. *Maracle is currently the Traditional Teacher for First Nations House and an instructor in the Aboriginal Studies Program, the Centre for Indigenous Theatre and S.A.G.E. [Support for Aboriginal Graduate Education].*

Sheila Sampath

Dear Sheila,

When you're in your 30s, you'll barely recognize the person you are now: while still gawky, awkward and (only sometimes) shy, you'll grow into a person you can feel okay about. You'll have good days and bad, and you'll make a *lot* of mistakes, but you'll recognize that you have a very tiny place in a very big world, and you'll do all that you can to make that matter.

Right now, you're managing alright, and you shouldn't understate the value in that. I know you don't know how to honour yourself just yet, but I honour you, and your choices, whenever I think about you. Your world feels huge, but it is situated in a much bigger one, and that's really what you are navigating. The things that you feel as *meanness* and *isolation* and *pain* are the systems of racism, sexism and classism playing out in your life. It's colonialism and it's patriarchy. It's *displacement*.

These are big things for a small person to understand, and I don't want to overwhelm you or alter the space-time continuum by suggesting that you change a *single thing*. I combed hard to think of regrets that I might have that you can avoid, but the best I could really come up with is to stop trying to tame your hair (it ain't gonna happen—plus, big hair is in again, eventually) and to stop thinking that avoiding the sun is going to make you any less brown (you'll come to terms with all this stuff—it's called *shadeism* and *internalized racism*—eventually). The truth is, you're going to mess up a lot, but it'll be good for us.

Your life isn't going to be perfect, and it's not going to be awesome, but it'll be okay, and for the most part, it'll feel good. When it doesn't, it'll feel good enough. Just so you know you're on the right track, and things are gonna be okay, here's a list of the top five things you have to look forward to, a lifetime (for you) down the road:

1. Community

You don't know what this means just yet, but you will. It's tied to all those -*isms* I mentioned earlier. At some point, those things will stop being the things that make you feel alone and will start being the things that make you feel the furthest from it. You'll discover a feeling of *connectedness* that comes from unpacking a lot of messy things. You'll do a lot of that, too; alone, and with other people.

2. Family

Your relationship with your family will change and grow into something really beautiful that you value deeply. Don't let this stop you from giving our mom a hard time. She'll come around, and so will you.

3. Music

All that time you spend hiding in your closet making mixtapes and reading music mags won't go to waste. This will be another place for you to find community and love and to take a break from all the very hard work that's ahead of you. One day, you'll tour in a *real, live band.* Actually, you'll play in a whole bunch of them, and you'll never get over how much fun that is. Thank our mom for the singing lessons, piano lessons and the karaoke tapes. (Oh, and that Pulp show you missed because of that poorly-scheduled science exam? You'll make up for it, twice over, in New York, in your 30s).

4. Best friends forever

That big group of people you eat lunch with every day? Well, you're not going to keep in touch with all of them (though you'll pretend to through this thing called *social networking,* which is equal parts amazing and horrifying—stay tuned). The ones you do keep in your life, you'll discover, are real superheroes. Like, just completely un-believable people who have strange powers, like a sixth sense to call on a bad day, or some kind of reactionary instinct that gets them to say *the* funniest thing at *exactly* the right time when you need to laugh the most, or the ability to just be *honest* and *real.* You'll grow apart for a while and then grow back together and there'll be all sorts of new and wonderful people added to the mix. They'll teach you a lot of things, too; take good notes and thank them often.

5. Superpowers

You have some superpowers, too, and you'll hone them carefully in your grown-up life. You are a lot more resilient than you think you are. And you know how to take something that feels earth-shatteringly awful and turn it into something that you can build. It's from forthcoming violence that you'll find yourself politicized in a Wednesday night open-session at a rape crisis centre. It's from feeling like everything that happens in the world is happening to you that will drive you to *learn* more and to *connect* and *make* and *act*. It's from the spaces of alienation and confusion that you feel now that you'll find yourself working countless hours on a feminist teen magazine and on this book. And it's in the voices of these amazing people within it that you'll find your own and write a letter you were once dreading to write.

And it's from all these things that you'll draw strength and humility and love and purpose. And you'll grow into a person who is always still growing, and feel as scared and excited as you do now about who that's going to be, another lifetime from now.

With love and respect,
Sheila

About Sheila

Sheila Sampath *is a Toronto-based designer and educator who has spent the last decade crafting creative for social good. She is the Principal and Creative Director at The Public, Editorial and Art Director of* Shameless Magazine *and teaches at the Ontario College of Art and Design University. Sheila is a member of the British Council's TN2020 network, a fellow of the Royal Society of Artists and has facilitated workshops and given lectures in strategic design, radical art and independent media internationally. She practices activism in all that she does and feels lucky to do it.*

Learn more about her work at <u>sheilasampath.ca</u>.

About Shameless

Shameless *is an award-winning, independent Canadian voice for smart, strong, sassy young women and trans youth. It's a fresh alternative to typical teen magazines, packed with articles about arts, culture and current events, reflecting the neglected diversity of our readers' interests and experiences. Grounded in principles of social justice and anti-oppression,* Shameless *aims to do more than just publish a magazine: we aim to inspire, inform and advocate for young women and trans youth.*

Shameless *strives to practice and develop an inclusive feminism. We understand that many of the obstacles faced by young women and trans youth lie at the intersection of different forms of oppression, based on race, class, ability, immigration status, sexual orientation and gender identity. As a grassroots magazine, we are committed to supporting and empowering young writers, editors, designers and artists, especially those from communities that are underrepresented in the mainstream media.*

Each issue of Shameless *entertains and inspires with profiles of amazing women and trans people, discussion of hot topics, DIY guides to crafty activities, sports dispatches, the latest in technology, columns on food politics, health and sexuality, advice and more.*

Proudly independent, Shameless *is published three times a year by a team of volunteer staff.*

For more information, visit <u>*shamelessmag.com*</u>*.*